FIFTY STORIES for 5 YEAR OLDS

Love to Alice
on her 5th birthday

Mommy & Daddy

FIFTY STORIES for 5 YEAR OLDS

Edited by
Marie Greenwood

Illustrated by
Annabel Spenceley

GALLERY BOOKS
An Imprint of W. H. Smith Publishers Inc.
112 Madison Avenue
New York City 10016

ACKNOWLEDGEMENTS

For permission to include copyright material,
acknowledgement and thanks are due to the following:

Donald Bisset for *A Journey to the Sea* from 'The Adventures of Yak'

Alice Ritchie for *Two of Everything* from 'The Treasure of Li-Po'

H. E. Todd and Hodder & Stoughton Ltd for *The Birds' Concert*

The Elephant and the Bad Baby by Elfrida Vipont, text © 1969
by Elfrida Vipont Foulds. Reprinted by permission of Coward-McCann, Inc.

Margaret Mahy and J. M. Dent & Sons Ltd for *A Lion in the Meadow*

Philippa Pearce for *Lion at School* © 1971 (Viking/Kestrel)

The following are reprinted by permission of Faber and Faber Ltd:

How the Polar Bear Became by Ted Hughes
from 'How the Whale Became and Other Stories'

Tim Rabbit's Magic Cloak by Alison Uttley
from 'Lavender Shoes: Eight Tales of Enchantment'

All other stories in this book are retold from traditional sources
by Nora Clarke and Linda Yeatman and in this version are © Grisewood & Dempsey Ltd

CONTENTS

THE ELVES
AND THE SHOEMAKER

O nce upon a time there was a shoemaker who made very good shoes. But though he worked hard in his shop, times were difficult and he became poorer and poorer. One evening he cut out some shoes from his last bit of leather and laid the pieces out on his workbench to sew in the morning when the light was better. He put everything ready including the needles and thread.

"I may never make another pair of shoes," he sighed as he put the shutters over his shop window. "When I finish and sell this pair, I must buy food for my family. Then there will be nothing left over to buy leather to make more shoes."

The next morning when he went over to his workbench, the first thing he saw was a beautiful pair of shoes. He examined them carefully and realized they were made from the leather he had cut out the night before. The stitches were exquisite, very tiny and neat, and he knew the shoes were far better than any he could have made. Quickly he took down his shutters and placed this fine pair of shoes in his shop window.

The shoemaker was still puzzling over who could have made the shoes when the door opened and in came a grand gentleman. He asked to buy the shoes he had seen in the window and paid four times more than the shoemaker had ever asked before for a pair of shoes. With this money the shoemaker bought more leather and enough food to feed the family for several days.

That evening he sat at his workbench and cut out two

8

pairs of shoes from his new leather. He left the pieces laid out as before, all ready to sew in the morning.

Then the shoemaker shut up the shop and went upstairs to join his family. In the morning he could scarcely believe his eyes, for there on his workbench were two beautiful pairs of shoes.

"Who could sew such tiny stitches?" he wondered, "And who could work so fast?"

He placed the shoes in the shop window. Rich people who had never visited his shop before came in to buy them, and paid a lot of money for them. The shoemaker took their money gladly, bought more leather and cut out more shoes.

Each night for many weeks the same thing happened. Two pairs, sometimes four pairs, were made in a night. The shoemaker became well-known for the excellent shoes he sold.

He cut out all sorts of shoes: men's shoes, ladies' shoes, party shoes, shoes with laces, shoes with straps, coloured shoes, little children's shoes, dancing shoes. Each week he took even more money in his shop and his family were happy and well fed at last.

One night his wife suggested they should peep around the door of the workroom to see if they could find out who their night visitors were. As the town clock struck midnight, there was a scuffling and a scurrying by the window, and two little men squeezed through a crack in the shutters and hurried over to the workbench. They took tiny tools from their workbags and began to work. For several hours they stitched and hammered, and before dawn a row of new shoes lay on the workbench. The shoemaker and his wife rubbed their eyes in disbelief, wondering if they were dreaming, for the little men were scarcely bigger than the shoemaker's needles. Then, their work finished, the elves left everything neat and tidy and vanished the way they had come.

As it was just before Christmas, the shoemaker's wife suggested that the next evening they should put out presents for the little men who had helped them so much during the year. All the next day she was busy making two little green jackets and trousers with green woollen hats to match while her husband stitched two tiny pairs of boots.

The shoemaker and his wife laid these gifts out on the workbench that evening together with two little glasses of

10

wine and plates with little cakes and biscuits. They then kept watch again. They saw the elves scramble into the workshop and climb on to the workbench as they had done before. When they saw the little green jackets, trousers and hats and tiny boots the elves gave a shout of joy. Immediately they tried on the clothes and they were so delighted they danced around the workbench, waving their hats in the air. They sat down and ate all the food that had been left out and disappeared as before.

After Christmas the shoemaker still cut out shoes and left the pieces on his workbench but the elves never returned. They knew the shoemaker and his wife must have spied them for their clothes were the exact size, and fairy people do not like to be seen by humans.

The shoemaker did not mind however, for his shop was now so well-known that he had plenty of customers. If the shoemaker's stitches were not as tiny and neat as the elves' stitches no one ever complained. Perhaps they never noticed. For many years he was known as the best shoemaker in town and he and his wife were never poor again. But they always remembered the elves and how they had been helped by them when times were hard.

THE WONDERFUL POT

In a little broken-down cottage there once lived a poor man and his wife. They had sold their furniture to buy food but they still had one cow. At last they had no money or food left so the man said he would take the cow to market and sell her.

He led her along the road where a stranger stopped him.

"Are you selling your fine cow?" he asked. "How much money will you take for her?"

"A hundred crowns," was the answer.

"I have no money," the stranger said, "but I will exchange this pot for your cow." He lifted up a black iron pot with three legs and a handle over the top.

"A pot!" the man cried. "My wife and children need food and I must have money to buy some. A pot is no use to me."

The two men stood in the road looking at each other and at the pot and the cow. Suddenly the pot shouted: "Take me!"

"If a pot can talk, it can do other things," the poor man thought so he handed over the cow to the stranger. Then he carried the pot home and put it in the cow-shed. He wanted to have a rest and something to eat but his wife met him in the doorway.

"Well," she said, "did you sell the cow at a good price?"

"Yes," he replied, "I'm pleased with the price."

"That's good. The money will be very useful."

"But dear wife, I didn't get any money. I got something useful which I left in the cow-shed."

His wife rushed outside. "How stupid!" she cried when she saw the pot. "How can I feed the children with an empty pot? I wish I'd taken the cow to market myself!"

She went on grumbling until the pot shouted: "Clean me, then put me on your fire."

"A talking pot! How wonderful!" the wife said, "If it can talk perhaps it can do other things." So she washed the pot and put it in the fire.

"I'm running! I'm running!" the pot laughed.

"Where are you running?" the woman asked.

"To the rich man, to the rich man," and the pot ran out of the kitchen and up the road on its three fat little legs.

The rich man's house was not far away and a lovely

smell of baking bread was coming from his kitchen. The pot jumped through the window and landed on the kitchen table.

"That's good," exclaimed the rich man's wife. "This pot is the right size for my pudding. It's just what I needed." And she started to mix lots of good things together – flour, butter, eggs, raisins, cherries and nuts. Soon the pot was full and she wanted to put it on the fire.

Tap, tap, tap. The pot had jumped to the door on its three short legs.

"Where are you going?" the woman asked.

"To the poor man's house," replied the pot and it raced back down the road.

"Look at this pudding, dear wife," said the husband. "Isn't this a good little pot?"

"Indeed it is," she replied and they all had a good meal that night.

Next morning the pot shouted: "I'm running, I'm running."

"Where are you running?" they asked.

"To the rich man's barn," it chuckled then it balanced on its three legs and away it ran.

It stood in the barn doorway and the rich man who was threshing wheat shouted: "Look at this odd little pot! How much wheat will it hold?"

He emptied a bag of wheat into it but it did not fill the pot. He poured in another bag, then another, but there was still plenty of room in the pot. The man went on pouring bag after bag until the barn was empty. At once, the pot ran outside.

"Stop!" the man shouted. "Where are you taking my wheat?"

"To the poor man's house," and the pot went thump, thump, thump, on its fat little legs all the way down the

road with the rich man running after it. "Stop, stop!" he cried, but the little pot soon reached the poor man's house.

"Husband, look at this!" the wife exclaimed. "This lovely little pot has filled our sheds with wheat. We won't be hungry for years."

They felt very happy and wondered what the pot would do next.

On the third morning the sun was shining brightly as the pot went along the road again with a hop, skip and a jump. The rich man was busy counting all his money on a table near the window. Many gold coins were glittering in the sun. The pot jumped through the open window and perched in the middle of them.

"I won't let this black pot get away from me this time," he said, "it will make a good money-box for me." Ten, fifty, a hundred coins he threw in, one after the other, until the table was empty. At that moment the pot jumped across to the window.

"Help! Thief! Robbers!" shouted the man, "Where are you going with all my gold?"

"To the poor man's house," sang the pot as it ran and did a funny little twirling dance all the way down the road.

The poor couple were speechless when the pot arrived with the gold. Then the husband said: "With this gold we can get a table, chairs, beds and clothes for the children."

"And another cow," his wife said with a laugh. "What a good exchange you made, dear husband."

"Please clean me well," was all the pot said.

On the fourth day the pot stood by the door. "I'm running, I'm running," it said.

"Where are you running?" the couple asked.

"To the rich man's house," and it tap, tap, tapped along the road and jumped into the rich man's kitchen once more. He was standing by the table when he spied the pot and he became very angry indeed.

"This is the horrid pot which took my wife's pudding, my wheat from the barn and all my gold. Give me back the things you stole or I'll break you into tiny pieces."

He threw himself over the pot but he could not get off again!

"I'm running, I'm running," sang the pot.

"Run to the North Pole if you want to!" screamed the rich man as he kicked and struggled. But the pot on its three fat little legs, turned and ran down the road with the man still on top. The poor man, his wife and children came outside but this time the pot did not stop.

No one ever knew if it did carry the man to the North Pole! The poor family was now the rich family and they often talked about the wonderful pot and all the things that it did but it never came back to visit them.

THE GINGERBREAD MAN

An old woman was baking one day, and she made some gingerbread. She had some dough left over, so she made the shape of a little man. She made eyes for him, a nose and a smiling mouth all of currants, and placed more currants down his front to look like buttons. Then she laid him on a baking tray and put him in the oven to bake.

After a little while, she heard something rattling at the oven door. She opened it and to her surprise out jumped the little gingerbread man she had made. She tried to catch him as he ran across the kitchen, but he slipped past her, calling as he ran:

"Run, run, as fast as you can,
You can't catch me, I'm the gingerbread man!"

She chased after him into the garden where her husband was digging. He put down his spade and tried to catch him too, but as the gingerbread man sped past him he called over his shoulder:

"Run, run, as fast as you can,
You can't catch me, I'm the gingerbread man!"

As he ran down the road he passed a cow. The cow called out, "Stop, gingerbread man! You look good to eat!" But the gingerbread man laughed and shouted over his shoulder:

"I've run from an old woman
And an old man.
Run, run, as fast as you can,
You can't catch me, I'm the gingerbread man!"

The cow ran after the old woman and the old man, and soon they all passed a horse. "Stop!" called out the horse, "I'd like to eat you." But the gingerbread man called out:

"I've run from an old woman
And an old man,
And a cow!
Run, run, as fast as you can,
You can't catch me, I'm the gingerbread man!"

He ran on, with the old woman and the old man and the cow and the horse following, and he went past a party of people haymaking. They all looked up as they saw the gingerbread man, and as he passed them he called out:

"I've run from an old woman,
And from an old man,
And a cow and a horse.
Run, run, as fast as you can,
You can't catch me, I'm the gingerbread man!"

The haymakers joined in the chase behind the old woman and the old man, the cow and the horse, and they all followed him as he ran through the fields. There he met a fox, so he called out to the fox:

"Run, run, as fast as you can,
You can't catch me, I'm the gingerbread man!"

But the sly fox said, "Why should I bother to catch you?" although he thought to himself, "That gingerbread man would be good to eat."

Just after he had run past the fox the gingerbread man had to stop because he came to a wide, deep, swift-flowing river. The fox saw the old woman and the old man, the cow, the horse and the haymakers all chasing the gingerbread man so he said,

"Jump on my back, and I'll take you across the river!"

The gingerbread man jumped on the fox's back and the fox began to swim. As they reached the middle of the river, where the water was deep, the fox said,

"Can you stand on my head, Gingerbread Man, or you will get wet." So the gingerbread man pulled himself up and stood on the fox's head. As the current flowed more swiftly, the fox said,

"Can you move on to my nose, Gingerbread Man, so that I can carry you more safely? I would not like you to drown." The gingerbread man slid on to the fox's nose. But when they reached the bank of the river, the fox suddenly went *snap*! The gingerbread man disappeared into the fox's mouth, and was never seen again.

THE GOLDEN GOOSE

In a faraway land years ago, there lived a couple who had three sons. The youngest boy was laughed at and teased by all the family for his foolish ways and they nicknamed him "Dum Dum".

One day, the eldest son took it into his head to go into the forest to chop firewood. His mother packed a delicious meat pie and a bottle of wine for him to take with him. At midday he sat down to eat and he had just opened his bag when a little old man passed by and called:

"Good day. Your food looks good. Will you give me a little piece of pie and a little of your wine, please? I'm very hungry and thirsty."

"What? Give away some pie and wine!" the eldest son said. "No, thank you. I shouldn't have enough for myself."

The little old man went away and the young man, who thought he had dealt with the old man very cleverly, went to chop up some logs. He had just got started when his axe slipped. He cut his leg badly and had to limp home. It was the little old man that had made his axe slip like that!

The second son went off to work next. His mother packed up a good dinner for him – a meat pie and a bottle of wine. The same little old man met him and asked for something to eat and drink. The second son thought he was cleverer than his brother so he called rudely:

"Whatever you get, means I get less. Be off with you!"
The little man walked away quietly but he made certain

that the second son got his reward. When he raised his axe a second time he hit himself on the foot and he went limping home as well!

Then Dum Dum said: "Father, I'd like to go and cut wood now."

"Your brothers have both hurt themselves," his father replied, "you know nothing about axes so you'd better stay at home."

Dum Dum begged so hard that at last his father said: "Go along, stupid. You'll learn your lesson, if you're hurt." His mother packed dry bread and sour beer for him!

He went off to the forest and when he was ready to eat, he met the same little old man.

"Give me some meat and a little wine," he asked as before.

"I've only got dry bread and sour beer," Dum Dum said, "but you're welcome to share it if you like. Let us sit down and eat together."

So they sat down. When the boy unpacked his bread it had turned into a beautiful crusty pie and the beer was now delicious wine. They ate and drank happily together. When they had finished the old man said:

"You have a kind heart and have shared everything with me so now I will give something to you. Can you see that old tree? Cut it down and you'll find something worth having at the root."

They shook hands and the old man went away.

Dum Dum's axe did not slip, so before long he had cut down the tree. When it fell, lo and behold, a goose with feathers of pure gold was sitting in a hollow under the roots. He picked the bird up and said to himself: "I shan't go home to be laughed at. I'll go and seek my fortune."

So off he went and later he came to an inn where the innkeeper had three daughters. When they saw the goose they were very curious about such a wonderful bird and they wanted to have one of its beautiful golden feathers. At last, the eldest daughter said:

"I *must* and *will* have a feather."

She waited until Dum Dum turned his back then she caught hold of the goose by its wing. But to her surprise, she couldn't pull her hand away.

Her second sister ran in to snatch a feather too.

"I'm stuck," whispered the eldest, "give me a pull." But the moment the second sister touched her, she stuck fast as well.

The third sister came along and the other two started screaming:

"Keep back. For heaven's sake, keep back!"

But she didn't, so all three sisters were stuck fast one behind the other, and behind the goose!

Later on, Dum Dum, taking no notice of the three screaming girls, picked up his goose and walked off. The girls had to follow whether they liked it or not, for they were stuck fast. If Dum Dum ran, they had to run as well.

He led them across a rough field where they met a parson. He wagged a finger at the girls. "Aren't you ashamed of yourselves, chasing after a young man like this? Is that good behaviour?"

The parson took hold of the youngest sister's hand to pull her away. The next moment, he stuck fast as well and had to run behind the little trail of people.

Presently the churchwarden came up and he wondered why the parson was running after the three girls. "Your Reverence," he said, "you're late for the christening at the church." He pulled the parson's sleeve. And he stuck fast! There were now five of them one behind

the other, following Dum Dum.

They met two labourers with shovels and the parson shouted to them: "Help! Come and set us free!"

The labourers tugged at the churchwarden's wide belt and, of course, they stuck fast too. This made seven people running after Dum Dum and his golden goose.

At last they arrived at a city which belonged to a king with one daughter. She never laughed or even smiled and her father proclaimed that whoever could make her laugh should have her for his wife.

As soon as Dum Dum heard this, he went to the palace with the goose under his arm, followed by all seven people. When the princess saw the seven hanging on together and treading on each other's heels, she thought they looked so funny that she couldn't help laughing. At once, Dum Dum claimed her for his wife. They were married and lived happily together thereafter.

Dum Dum was not so stupid after all, was he?

THE WISHING RING

There was once a young man who had a small farm. He and his wife were very poor although they worked hard from morning until night.

One day he was ploughing his little field and he sat down for a rest as it was hard work. "I must sell half this field," he said sadly, "for we have no money left. Oh, what will become of my wife and children?"

Suddenly an old woman dressed all in black, crept up and tapped him on his shoulder.

"Young man," she said, "it's no good sitting there feeling sorry for yourself. Take my advice and do something about it. Follow your nose for two days wherever it takes you through the forest. You will come to a tall pine tree, taller than any tree you've ever seen. If you can cut it down by yourself, good fortune will come to you." Then she vanished.

The farmer rushed to get his axe and some food then he set off. It took him two days to find the tree and at once he started to chop the huge tree trunk. It fell to the ground with a mighty crash and a bird's nest with two eggs in it tumbled out of the branches. The eggs cracked and broke as they rolled out of the nest. A fluffy baby eagle crawled out of one shell and a gold ring fell out of the other.

To the farmer's surprise, the eagle started to grow, and in a few seconds it reached his waist. It stretched and flapped its big wings and cried, "You have set me free! Please take this gold ring as a reward. Take care of it for it is a wishing ring. You put it on your finger, turn it round

26

and make a wish. But remember, there is only one wish in the ring. Once you wish, the ring loses it magic. So think carefully what you would like – you don't want to waste your wish."

The eagle looked wonderful as it rose into the sky. It swooped down once more and slowly flapped its wings then it shot away and disappeared into the clouds.

The farmer picked up the ring and walked on. It was too late to reach home that night so he decided to stay in the nearby town. He saw a goldsmith's shop with many gold rings to sell, so he went inside.

"How much would you say my ring was worth?" he asked.

"Only a few coins," the goldsmith replied.

"It is worth a lot more to me," the farmer laughed. "It is a wishing ring and it is worth more than all the rings you have here."

The shopkeeper was a cunning rascal. "Why don't you spend the night here in my spare room?" he said.

But as soon as the farmer fell asleep the goldsmith crept in, took the wishing ring and left another gold ring there instead.

The goldsmith wanted to get rid of the farmer quickly so early next morning he shook him awake. "You'd better get up now for you have a long walk to get to your house."

As soon as the farmer walked away, the rascal closed the shutters. He bolted the heavy door and stood in the middle of the room. He turned the ring on his finger and said:

"I wish for a million gold coins."

At once coins fell like hard shiny raindrops. They hit him on his head and shoulders and he yelled with pain. They covered the floor and soon they were up to his knees.

27

He rushed to unbolt the door. Too late! He could not run through the gold and soon he was covered up. Thousands of coins fell and they were so heavy that the floor broke and the wicked shopkeeper went crashing to the ground. The gold kept on tumbling down until one million coins lay there. But the greedy goldsmith never got up again for he was buried under the mountain of gold.

In the meantime, the farmer got back to his house and he showed the ring, which he thought was the wishing ring, to his wife.

"This will make our fortune," he said, "but we must be careful. Our wish must be a good one!"

"Let us wish for some more fields," said his wife.

"We need more land, it is true," her husband replied, "but if we work really hard for a year, perhaps we could buy the fields next door."

All that year the farmer and his wife worked in the fields. The weather was good so their crops grew and the corn grew tall and strong. He sold the corn in the market and with that money, he bought the two fields next door to his farm.

"This is wonderful," he told his wife. "We have the land we wanted and I have a little money left over. And we haven't used our wish either!"

"What about wishing for a horse and a cow?" his wife asked. "They would be useful to us."

"We bought the fields with our own money, dear wife. It won't take us long to get enough for a horse and cow."

So they worked hard and in quite a short time they saved enough to buy a strong horse and a beautiful cow.

"Aren't we lucky," said the farmer. "We have three fields, a horse to ride and a cow to give us good milk. We have everything we want! And we still have our wish from the ring."

"Why don't we get a new house?" his wife asked. "I'd like a garden with a pretty pond and some ducks to swim on it."

"We must not be in a hurry to use the wish, my dear, for that is the only wish we can have," and he went off to the fields whistling merrily.

His wife kept running to him whenever she wanted to make a wish but somehow he never wanted to wish for the same things! One day she said to him: "It's funny to hear you singing so happily in the fields. You used to grumble and work very hard when we were poor. Why don't you take a rest? You needn't work. You could wish for a big farm; you could be a king; you could fill the barns with gold! You could get anything with that ring but I think you can't make up your mind!"

"I wish you wouldn't think about the ring so much," her husband replied. "I am still young and strong and I like working in our fields. We grow good crops, we have plenty of food, our children are happy and we have saved some money as well. It is better to save the wishing ring until we really need it."

"Very well, husband," she said, "all the same I can't help wondering what to wish for."

The couple did not tell their children about the ring but sometimes they joked about it to each other.

And so the farmer and his wife lived in great happiness for the rest of their lives. They were often tempted to use the ring, but never did, so they never found out that it was just an ordinary ring.

THE FISHERMAN AND HIS WIFE

There was once a fisherman who lived with his wife in a tumble-down cottage near the sea. It had only one room. The windows were broken and the rain poured through the roof when it rained. The husband went out fishing every day but he did not catch many fish so they never had much money.

One day when the sun was sparkling on the waves, the fisherman was watching his fishing lines when one of them was dragged into deep water. Slowly he managed to pull the line up and on the hook was an enormous fish! To the fisherman's astonishment it rolled its eyes and started to speak.

"Don't kill me," it said, "please let me swim away."

"Goodness me," said the man, "I don't want to eat a talking fish! I'll let you go as soon as I can."

He caught hold of the fish and gently took the hook out of its mouth. The fish swished its tail and darted straight to the bottom of the sea.

The fisherman did not catch another fish all day. He had nothing to sell so he went home. The sun disappeared and it poured with rain. As he dried himself he told his wife what had happened.

"I'm glad I let the talking fish go," he said.

"Didn't you ask this fish for anything?" his wife asked.

"No," said the man, "what should I have asked for?"

"Oh husband," the wife spoke crossly, "the fire smokes, the roof leaks, the window has no glass and we

31

have no food! Why not tell the fish you spared his life so now you want a nice little reward?''

The man didn't want to go but his wife kept telling him what he should do, so in the end he went to the shore.

The sea was no longer sparkling. It was grey but smooth and the fisherman shivered as he stood by the water's edge and called:

"Great Fish in the Sea,
Come here to me, I pray,
My wife demands her wish, you see,
Before the end of day.''

At once, the water bubbled and the big fish came swimming towards him. It lifted up its head and said:

"What does your wife wish for?''

"Well,'' the man replied, "she says that when I caught you I should have asked for something before I let you go. We live in a small, damp hut and she wants to live in a proper little cottage.''

"Go home then,'' said the fish, "she is in her cottage already.''

The fisherman rushed back. His wife was standing in the doorway of a pretty cottage. He could see a garden filled with flowers and vegetables, a pond with ducks swimming in it and grass where hens and chickens clucked busily.

"Come in, come in,'' she called, "this is much better than our old hut!''

The husband was overjoyed. "How happy we will be in this dear little home,'' he said.

For a few weeks everything went well but the fisherman noticed that his wife looked cross about

something when he came back from his fishing. She started to grumble.

"There isn't enough room for our furniture," she said. "I'd like a rose-garden and the hens need more grass."

He didn't take any notice at first, then every night she started saying the same thing. "Why can't we live in a stone castle? You should go to the fish again. Tell it to give us a fine castle!"

"I don't want to do that," said her husband, "I'm happy with this cottage. Besides, the fish might be annoyed."

"Nonsense," his wife replied, "it'll be happy to help us. Just you wait and see. Go along and try!"

At last the man went to the shore again. The water

was calm but it looked grey and threatening and a chilly wind blew. He called fearfully:

> *"Great Fish in the Sea,*
> *Come here to me, I pray,*
> *My wife demands her wish, you see,*
> *Before the end of day."*

Swish! And the fish appeared.

"What does she want now?" it said.

"I'm afraid she wants to live in a stone castle," the fisherman replied. His face was worried.

"Go home then," the fish said, "she is in the castle already."

Away he ran. He found his wife standing by a stone archway which led into a wonderful castle.

"What did I tell you!" she laughed, "The fish helped gladly. Just look at this grand castle!"

They went inside together. There were servants everywhere ready to look after them. The rooms were full of golden furniture, velvet cushions and curtains, gleaming mirrors and blazing fires. Behind the castle there were gardens, woods and meadows. In the stables were horses and carriages.

"Gracious me," said the man, "what a wonderful palace. We can live happily here for the rest of our lives!"

"Let us wait and see," said his wife.

The servants carried in a grand supper and after that, the couple went upstairs and had a good sleep.

But it wasn't long before the wife began to grumble again.

"I want us to be king and queen of all the land," she said. "Go and talk to the fish and tell him what I say."

"How can you be queen?" her husband exclaimed, "And I'm sure I don't want to be king!"

"Well, I still want to be queen," said his wife, "so you'd better think about seeing the fish again."

She scolded and badgered her husband so much that he grew tired of listening so he went to the shore. The sea was rough. Waves crashed down as he cried:

> *"Great Fish in the Sea,*
> *Come here to me, I pray,*
> *My wife demands her wish, you see,*
> *Before the end of day."*

"What does she want?" the fish said as it swam through the heavy waves.

"She wants to be queen and to rule over everybody. But I don't want to be king, whatever she does!"

"Go home then," said the fish, "she is queen already."

The man walked back slowly. Soon he heard drums and trumpets and he saw soldiers marching up and down in front of a palace which was far grander than the stone castle. He went past the smart guards at the gate and into the Great Hall. He saw his wife sitting on a high throne of gold and diamonds. She was wearing a shining crown and many servants waited to help her.

"Well, wife," said the fisherman, "are you head of all the land now?"

"Yes," she said, "I am the queen!"

The man was sure that his wife could not wish for anything more, so he was happy and contented.

Then to his horror, his wife found out that an emperor was more important than a queen so she sent for her husband and said to him:

"I'm tired of being queen. Go to the fish and tell it I must be an emperor!"

The poor man was miserable. "I can't go," he said.

"I am your queen," said his wife, "I order you to go at once."

So once more he trailed off to the shore. The water looked dark and dangerous. The wind was blowing hard and waves thundered onto the sand. There was so much noise that the fisherman had to shout his message:

"Great Fish in the Sea,
Come here to me, I pray,
My wife demands her wish, you see,
Before the end of day."

36

The fish lifted its head above the huge waves.

"What does she want now?" it said.

"Oh dear," the man said fearfully, "she wants to be emperor."

"Go home then," the fish said, "she is emperor already."

When he got to the palace he saw his wife perched on a much higher throne, wearing a diamond crown as tall as herself! Hundreds of servants stood behind her, and kings, princes and nobles were kneeling or bowing as the fisherman went to her throne and said:

"Well, wife, are you emperor?"

"Yes," she replied. "I am emperor!"

The fisherman was not happy in that grand palace. He hoped his wife had got all she wanted now. But, oh dear, that very night she called to him:

"I've decided that it isn't enough to be emperor. I want to have power over the sun and moon."

The poor fisherman was shocked. "How can you want such a thing! No living person can rule over the sun and moon."

"That is what you think," she replied, "I have made up my mind. Tomorrow you must see this fish again."

"But the fish cannot grant such a wish," he said.

"I order you to go," she said. "We'd still be poor and hungry in that wretched old hut if I hadn't used my brains. Order the fish to obey me!"

The fisherman argued but his wife shouted and screamed so much that at last he was worn out with arguing and agreed to go.

Next morning as he walked miserably to the shore a terrible storm arose. The howling winds were shaking the trees and a big branch just missed hitting him. The sky was filled with black clouds and enormous waves crashed down upon the beach. The storm was so fierce that boats were tossing and bouncing in the waves like little balls. The fisherman was shivering with fear. He was sure a wave might knock him over so he gritted his teeth and crept as close as he dared. He shouted but his voice was drowned by the noise of crashing waves and roaring winds:

> *"Great Fish in the Sea,*
> *Come here to me, I pray,*
> *My wife demands her wish, you see,*
> *Before the end of day."*

Lightning flashed. Thunder crashed. The fish appeared!

"What does she want now?" said the fish.

"I'm afraid she wants to rule the sun and moon," the fisherman said in a quivery voice.

The fish seemed to stand on its tail.

"Go home then," it said. "Go home and see."

The fisherman trailed away, wet, cold and wretched. In front of him he saw their old tumble-down hut and there he and his wife had to live for the rest of their lives.

The Miller, His Son and Their Donkey

One day a miller and his son were taking their donkey to the market to sell him.

On the road they met some girls who were laughing and chattering. "Just look at this silly couple!" the girls exclaimed. "Why are they walking along this dusty road when they could ride?"

"They are right," said the miller, "so up you get, my son, and I'll walk by your side."

Presently they met some old friends, so they stopped to talk.

"You should be riding on that donkey," they told him, "not tiring yourself out. Your son is a real lazybones. Make him walk. It will do him good."

So the miller changed places with his son whose legs soon became tired.

They had not gone far when they met a large band of women and children. The miller was startled when they began to scold him.

"What a selfish fellow you are," they cried. "Fancy riding along so comfortably and making your poor little boy trudge behind you! Can't you see that he is tired out?"

The miller at once lifted the boy up and they rode on together.

After a time they came across a band of travellers.

"Is that your own donkey?" they asked the miller, "Or have you borrowed it from a friend?"

"It belongs to me," the miller replied. "I'm taking

him to the market to sell."

"Goodness gracious," they said, "the poor thing will be worn out by carrying the two of you and nobody will want to buy it. You'd better carry it the rest of the way."

"We'll try that," said the miller. "Thank you for your good advice!"

They got off the donkey and tied his legs together with a rope. Then they slung him on a pole and carried him into the town.

When the townsfolk saw the miller and his son struggling to carry the donkey they burst out laughing. "How stupid! Whoever heard of carrying a donkey!" they called. There was so much noise that the poor donkey twisted and kicked and broke the ropes round his legs. He rushed through the streets and out of the town and was never seen again.

"I did what everybody told me," the miller said sadly as he went home, "and in the end I lost my poor donkey. I wish I'd stayed at home!"

THE LITTLE HOUSE

Once upon a time a large earthenware jar rolled off the back of a cart that was going to market. It came to rest in the grass at the side of the road.

By and by a mouse came along and looked at the jar. "What a fine house that would make," he thought, and he called out:

"Little house, little house,
Who lives in the little house?"

Nobody answered so the mouse peeped in and saw that it was empty. He moved in straight away and began to live there.

Before long a frog came by and saw the jar. "What a fine house that would make," he thought, and he called out:

"Little house, little house,
Who lives in the little house?"
and he heard:

"I, Mr Mouse.
I live in the little house.
Who are you?"

"I am Mr Frog," came the reply.

"Come in Mr Frog, and we can live here together," called out the mouse.

So the mouse and the frog lived happily together in the little house. Then one day a hare came running along the road and saw the little house. He called out:

"Little house, little house,
Who lives in the little house?"

41

and he heard:

"Mr Frog and Mr Mouse,
We live in the little house.
Who are you?"

"I am Mr Hare," he replied.

"Come in Mr Hare and live with us," called the mouse and the frog.

The hare went in and settled down with the frog and the mouse in the little house.

Some time later a fox came along, and spied the little house. "That would make a fine house," he thought and he called out:

"Little house, little house,
Who lives in the little house?"
and he heard:

"Mr Hare, Mr Frog and Mr Mouse,
We all live in the little house.
Who are you?"

"I am Mr Fox," he replied.

"Then come in and live with us, Mr Fox," they called.

Mr Fox went in and found there was just room for him too, although it was a bit of a squeeze.

The next day a bear came ambling along the road, and saw the little house. He called out:

"Little house, little house,
Who lives in the little house?"
and he heard:

"Mr Fox, Mr Hare, Mr Frog and Mr Mouse,
We all live in the little house.
Who are you?"

"I am Mr Bear Squash-you-all-flat," said the bear.

He then sat down on the little house, and squashed it all flat. That was the end of the little house.

JACK AND THE
BEANSTALK

There was once a boy called Jack who was brave and quick-witted. He lived with his mother in a small cottage and their most valuable possession was their cow, Milky-White. But the day came when Milky-White gave them no milk and Jack's mother said she must be sold.

"Take her to market," she told Jack, "and mind you get a good price for her."

So Jack set out to market leading Milky-White by her halter. After a while he sat down to rest by the side of the road. An old man came by and Jack told him where he was going.

"Don't bother to go to the market," the old man said. "Sell your cow to me. I will pay you well. Look at these beans. Only plant them, and overnight you will find you have the finest bean plants in all the world. You'll be better off with these beans than with an old cow or money. Now, how many is five, Jack?"

"Two in each hand and one in your mouth," replied Jack, as sharp as a needle.

"Right you are, here are five beans," said the old man and he handed the beans to Jack and took Milky-White's halter.

When he reached home, his mother said, "Back so soon, Jack? Did you get a good price for Milky-White?"

Jack told her how he had exchanged the cow for five beans and before he could finish his account, his mother started to shout and box his ears. "You lazy good-for-nothing boy!" she screamed, "How could you hand over

43

our cow for five old beans?
What will we live on now?
We shall starve to death,
you stupid boy."

She flung the beans
through the open window
and sent Jack to bed without
his supper.

When Jack woke the next
morning there was a strange
green light in his room. All
he could see from the window was green leaves. A
huge beanstalk had shot up
overnight. It grew higher
than he could see. Quickly
Jack got dressed and stepped out of the window right
onto the beanstalk and
started to climb.

"The old man said the beans would grow overnight," he thought. "They must indeed be very special beans."

Higher and higher Jack climbed until at last he reached the top and found himself on a strange road. Jack followed it until he came to a great castle where he could smell the most delicious breakfast. Jack was hungry. It had been a long climb and he had had nothing to eat since midday the day before. Just as he reached the door of the castle he nearly tripped over the feet of an enormous woman.

"Here, boy," she called. "What are you doing? Don't you know my husband likes to eat boys for breakfast? It's lucky I have already fried up some bacon and mushrooms for him today, or I'd pop you in the frying pan. He can eat you tomorrow, though."

"Oh, please don't let him eat me," pleaded Jack. "I only came to ask you for a bite to eat. It smells so delicious."

Now the giant's wife had a kind heart and did not really enjoy cooking boys for breakfast, so she gave Jack a bacon sandwich. He was still eating it when the ground began to shake with heavy footsteps, and a loud voice boomed: "Fee, Fi, Fo, Fum."

"Quick, hide!" cried the giant's wife and she pushed Jack into the oven. "After breakfast, he'll fall asleep," she whispered. "That is when you must creep away." She left the oven door open a crack so that Jack could see into the room. Again the terrible rumbling voice came:

"Fee, Fi, Fo, Fum,
I smell the blood of an Englishman,
Be he alive or be he dead,
I'll grind his bones to make my bread."

A huge giant came into the room. "Boys, boys, I smell boys," he shouted. "Wife, have I got a boy for breakfast today?"

"No, dear," she said soothingly. "You have got bacon and mushrooms. You must still be smelling the boy you ate last week."

The giant sniffed the air suspiciously but at last sat down. He wolfed his breakfast of bacon and mushrooms, drank a great bucketful of steaming tea and crunched up a massive slice of toast. Then he fetched a couple of bags of gold from a cupboard and started counting gold coins. Before long he dropped off to sleep.

Quietly Jack crept out of the oven. Carefully he picked up two gold coins and ran as fast as he could to the top of the beanstalk. He threw the gold down to his mother's garden and climbed after it. At the bottom he found his mother looking in amazement at the gold coins and the beanstalk. Jack told her of his adventures in the giant's castle and when she examined the gold she realized he must be speaking the truth.

Jack and his mother used the gold to buy food. But the day came when the money ran out, and Jack decided to climb the beanstalk again.

It was all the same as before, the long climb, the road to the castle, the smell of breakfast and the giant's wife. But she was not so friendly this time.

"Aren't you the boy who was here before," she asked, "on the day that some gold was stolen from under my husband's nose?"

But Jack convinced her she was wrong and in time her heart softened again and she gave him some breakfast. Once more as Jack was eating the ground shuddered and the great voice boomed: "'Fee, Fi, Fo, Fum." Quickly,

Jack jumped into the oven.

As he entered, the giant bellowed:

> "Fee, Fi, Fo, Fum,
> I smell the blood of an Englishman,
> Be he alive or be he dead,
> I'll grind his bones to make my bread."

The giant's wife put a plate of sizzling sausages before him, telling him he must be mistaken. After breakfast the giant fetched a hen from a back room. Every time he said "Lay!" the hen laid an egg of solid gold.

"I must steal that hen, if I can," thought Jack, and he waited until the giant fell asleep. Then he slipped out of the oven, snatched up the hen and ran for the top of the beanstalk. Keeping the hen under one arm, he scrambled down as fast as he could.

Jack's mother was waiting but she was not pleased when she saw the hen.

"Another of your silly ideas, is it, bringing an old hen when you might have brought us some gold? I don't know, what is to be done with you?"

Then Jack set the hen down carefully, and commanded "Lay!" just as the giant had done. To his mother's surprise the hen laid an egg of solid gold.

Jack and his mother now lived in great luxury. But in time Jack became a little bored and decided to climb the beanstalk again.

This time he did not risk talking to the giant's wife in case she recognized him. He slipped into the kitchen when she was not looking, and hid himself in the log basket. He watched the giant's wife prepare breakfast and then he heard the giant's roar:

"Fee, Fi, Fo, Fum,
I smell the blood of an Englishman,
Be he alive or be he dead,
I'll grind his bones to make my bread."

"If it's that cheeky boy who stole your gold and our magic hen, then I'll help you catch him," said the giant's wife. "Why don't we look in the oven? It's my guess he'll be hiding there."

You may be sure that Jack was glad he was not in the oven. The giant and his wife hunted high and low but never thought to look in the log basket. At last they gave up and the giant sat down to breakfast.

After he had eaten, the giant fetched a harp. When he commanded "Play!" the harp played the most beautiful music. Soon the giant fell asleep, and Jack crept out of the log basket. Quickly he snatched up the harp and ran. But

the harp called out loudly, "Master, save me! Save me!" and the giant woke. With a roar of rage he chased after Jack.

Jack raced down the road towards the beanstalk with the giant's footsteps thundering behind him. When he reached the top of the beanstalk he threw down the harp and started to slither down after it. The giant followed, and now the whole beanstalk shook and shuddered with his weight, and Jack feared for his life. At last he reached the ground, and seizing an axe he chopped at the beanstalk with all his might. *Snap!*

"Look out, mother!" he called as the giant came tumbling down, head first. He lay dead at their feet with the beanstalk on the ground beside them. The harp was broken, but the hen continued to lay golden eggs for Jack and his mother and they lived happily for a long, long time.

THE GREAT BIG TURNIP

Once upon a time, in Russia, an old man planted some turnip seeds. Each year he grew good turnips, but this year he was especially proud of one very big turnip. He left it in the ground longer than the others and watched with amazement and delight as it grew bigger and bigger. It grew so big that no one could remember ever having seen such a huge turnip before.

At last it stopped growing, and the old man decided that the time had come to pull it up. He took hold of the leaves of the great big turnip and pulled and pulled, but the turnip did not move.

So the old man called his wife to come and help him. The old woman pulled the old man, and the old man pulled the turnip. Together they pulled and pulled, but

50

the turnip did not move.

So the old woman called her granddaughter to come and help. The granddaughter pulled the old woman, the old woman pulled the old man, and the old man pulled the turnip. Still the turnip did not move.

The granddaughter called to the dog to come and help. The dog pulled the granddaughter, the granddaughter pulled the old woman, the old woman pulled the old man, and the old man pulled the turnip. But the great big turnip stayed firmly in the ground.

The dog called to the cat to come and help pull up the turnip. The cat pulled the dog, the dog pulled the granddaughter, the granddaughter pulled the old woman, the old woman pulled the old man, and the old man pulled the turnip. They all pulled and pulled as hard as they could, but still the turnip did not move.

Then the cat called to a mouse to come and help pull up the great big turnip. The mouse pulled the cat, the cat pulled the dog, the dog pulled the granddaughter, the granddaughter pulled the old woman, the old woman pulled the old man, and he pulled the big turnip. Together they pulled and pulled and pulled as hard as they could.

Suddenly, the great big turnip came out of the ground, and everyone fell over.

A JOURNEY TO THE SEA

Yak was waiting for the morning. He heard the tinkling of a bell in the monastery, nearby.

Every morning, while it was still dark, he could hear it. Small white snowflakes fell out of the dark on to his long warm hair. Gradually the sun rose. For a moment all was still. Then, out of the greyness floated a seagull.

"Yark!" it cried.

"Mrmph!" replied Yak.

Which is a sound very like English cows make while they are waiting in the meadows to be taken home at milking time.

Mocka, the seagull, landed on a rock close by.

Now it was morning.

Mocka was Yak's friend, who lived by the sea.

How Yak longed to go to the seaside. Mocka had told him about the children with buckets and spades on the beach. About the waves that rolled ashore every moment, hour after hour, day after day, year after year for a thousand million years, way beyond the edge of time.

Mocka hopped from the rock and laid something among the stones by Yak's hooves.

It was a sea-shell. A lovely spiral sea-shell.

"For me?" Yak looked at him. He put his ear by the shell and heard, as from far away, the hiss and murmur of the sea.

"Yark!" went Mocka – and flew away. Yak tilted his head and hooked the shell on to one of his horns. Then pressed it lightly against a rock so that it held firm.

He felt another Yak close by, and knew it was his mother.

She licked him.

"Yaks can't go to the seaside, Yak," she said. "It's much too far away. And you'd get lost."

Mocka was a speck in the distance.

"Perhaps I could follow Mocka," said Yak. "He passes every morning on his way to the sea."

His mother ate some grass.

Yak wandered down the hill. He crossed a mountain stream, stepping on the stones.

"Hello, Yak! Hello, Yak!" called the stream. "Look at me! Look at me! I'm going to the seaside."

Yak stumbled on a stone and fell *splash* into the water.

He didn't mind. It was rather fun being carried along by the stream. He lay on his back and watched the sun rise. Then he shut his eyes. It felt funny moving without seeing where he was going, yet rather nice. So he stayed like that.

When he opened his eyes again, the river, now no longer a stream, was flowing gently. The sun was overhead. A heron was standing in the water. As Yak floated by, it stared after him. It had never seen a yak floating down the river before.

"Well," thought the heron, "he's going to get to the seaside soon." He flapped his wings and flew after Yak, who had turned over and was swimming now.

"Mrmph!" Yak called to the heron – it was difficult making Mrmphing noises in the water. "Mrmphlp gulp – where am I?"

The heron didn't hear him, and flew away. Yak was alone on the wide, wide river.

He could feel the shell on his horn. Waves rippled

against him. He felt strangely contented. He lapped the water. It was salty!

"Salt!" thought Yak.

"Sea!" thought Yak. Mocka had told him that the sea was salty. He turned over on his back, again, and drifted.

"Shall I shut my eyes again?" he thought. "Shall I keep them shut and see?"

"How can I see if they're shut? I am a silly Yak!"

Yak sometimes talked to himself like this inside his head.

"I mean," he thought, "see what HAPPENS. It's a sort of 'See what happens' day." So he shut his eyes.

He could hear a boat go "chug chug chug" as it passed, in the distance.

Yak floated on.

Next time he opened his eyes, the sun was further across the sky and Yak felt hungry. So he paddled towards the shore and climbed the river bank and ate

some grass. There was a strange smell in the air. And a noise.

He'd heard that noise before in his shell.

He stumbled hurriedly through the grass.

He climbed a hill.

There, ahead, was a vast expanse of water.

Yak gazed at it for a long time. All around, the sky and the sea touched, and the waves sparkled in the sunshine.

To his right, on the yellow sand, some children were watching something.

Yak went to look.

It was a Punch and Judy show. Mocka had told him about those. He stayed to watch.

Presently a man with an ice-cream cart came by.

"Lovely ice-a-creams!" he called. "Ten-a-pence each!"

The children bought some. Yak went on following the

man, who stopped and looked at him. Then he smiled and gave Yak an ice-cream.

Lick – "Oh yum!" Yak liked it very much.

They walked on, together. In the distance were some rocks.

"You-a go-a long-a there-a, Yak-a," said the man.

He was an Italian man.

"You go-a long-a there, and find-a nice-a cave-a." He lifted his hat and said goodbye.

"Mrmph!" went Yak, and walked till he came to the rocks. It was quiet there.

Yak did find a cave. A nice dry cave. He rested and looked at the sea.

"I'm at the seaside!" he thought. "Really at the seaside!"

The waves rolled ashore – minute after minute, hour after hour, nearer and nearer, rolling among the pebbles and sand, as Yak lay watching.

A big ship, tiny in the distance, crept, like a snail, across the horizon.

Some seagulls flew about, mewing as they played.

Yak looked, but Mocka wasn't among them.

Presently it began to grow dark.

Then darker and darker.

The moon rose and all was still, save for the sound of the waves breaking on the shore.

Yak listened to his shell, again. It made exactly the same noise as the sea.

What a day it had been! He had come such a long way and seen so many new things.

He listened to his shell just once more. Then curled up so that his warm hair covered his nose and his legs, and soon fell fast asleep.

THE THREE WISHES

One day a poor woodcutter was working in the forest chopping down trees and sawing them into logs. He stopped for a moment and saw a fairy sitting on a leaf nearby. He closed his eyes, he rubbed them, but she was still there.

"I have come," she told him, "to give you three wishes. The next three wishes you make will come true. Use them wisely." With that she vanished.

After work, the woodcutter returned home and told his wife what had happened. She did not believe a word he said.

"You've just dreamt it," she laughed. "Still, just in case, you'd better think carefully before you wish."

Together they wondered. Should they wish for gold, jewels, a fine home? They argued and disagreed about everything until the woodcutter shouted crossly,

"I'm hungry after all my work. Let's eat first."

"I'm afraid there's only soup," his wife replied. "I'd no money to buy any meat."

"Soup again!" grumbled the woodcutter. "How I wish that we had a fine fat sausage to eat tonight."

Before they could blink, a fine fat sausage appeared on their kitchen table.

"You idiot!" screeched his wife. "Now you've wasted one of our precious wishes. You make me so angry." She went on scolding until he could stand it no more and he shouted,

"I wish that sausage was on the end of your nose!"

Immediately the large sausage jumped in the air and attached itself to the wife's nose. There she stood at the table with the big fat sausage hanging down in front of her. It was difficult to talk with it hanging there and she became really angry when the woodcutter laughed at her because she looked so ridiculous. She pulled and pulled; he pulled and pulled. But the sausage stayed there, stuck on the end of her nose.

The woodcutter soon stopped laughing when he remembered they only had one of the fairy's wishes left.

"Let's wish," he said quickly, "for all the riches in the world."

"What good would that do," she asked, "with a long sausage hanging from my nose? I could not enjoy them for one minute! People would laugh at me wherever I went."

The woodcutter and his wife finally agreed that they could do nothing except get rid of that sausage-nose.

The woodcutter wished and in a flash the sausage was gone, and he and his wife sat down to eat the soup that she had prepared for their supper. The only point they could agree on for a long while was how foolish they had both been to use the fairy's wishes so unwisely. They also wished – too late by now – that they had eaten the sausage when it had first appeared.

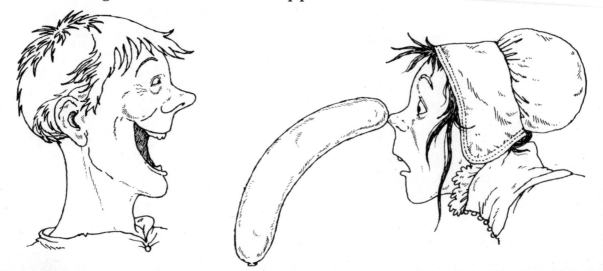

LITTLE RED RIDING HOOD

There was once a pretty little girl who lived in a cottage on the edge of a wood. Her grandmother who lived at the other side of the wood had made her a warm red cape with a hood, and as she often wore it, she became known as Little Red Riding Hood.

One day her mother called her and said, "Little Red Riding Hood, will you take this basket of food to your grandmother as she isn't very well. Carry the basket carefully for I have filled it with some cakes, some fresh bread and some butter."

So Little Red Riding Hood put on her red cape and carrying the basket carefully she set off through the wood to her grandmother's house. As she went, she wandered off the path to pick some pretty flowers and to look at some butterflies. Then, quite unexpectedly, she met a wolf.

The wolf licked his lips when he saw the pretty little girl. But he could not risk eating her there as he could hear some woodmen working in a clearing close by.

"Where are you going, little girl?" he asked instead.

"I'm going to my grandmother," Little Red Riding Hood answered, "I have some presents for her as she is ill."

"And where does your grandmother live?" asked the wolf, thinking if he was clever he might be able to eat the little girl *and* her grandmother.

"Through the wood, and her's is the first cottage you can see," replied Little Red Riding Hood. She went on

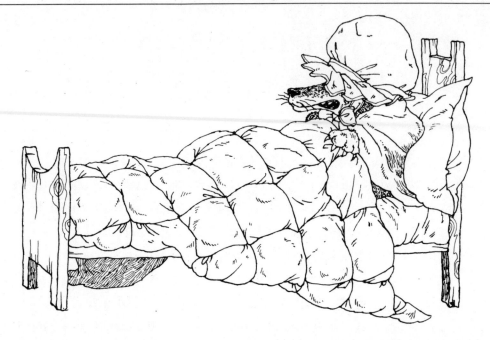

slowly through the wood, stopping here and there to add some more flowers to the bunch she was holding. The wolf watched her for a few minutes. Then he ran by the shortest route through the trees to the grandmother's cottage.

When he arrived there he knocked at the door.

"Who is there?" he heard an old lady call.

"It is me, Little Red Riding Hood, grandmother, with some presents for you," answered the wicked wolf, making his voice sound as much like Little Red Riding Hood's as he could.

"Pull the bobbin and the latch will go up," called the old lady from her bed.

The wolf pulled the bobbin, the latch went up, and he bounded into the room. In a trice he had gobbled up the poor old lady. He then put on her shawl and nightcap and got into her bed to wait for Little Red Riding Hood.

In a while there was a knock at the door.

"Who is there?" quavered the wolf, trying to make his voice sound as much like the old lady's as possible.

"It's me, Little Red Riding Hood," answered the girl. "I have brought you some food from my mother."

"Pull the bobbin and the latch will go up," called the wolf. The voice sounded rather gruff to Little Red Riding Hood.

She thought it must be because her grandmother had a sore throat. The wolf tugged the bedclothes up as far as he could under his chin as Little Red Riding Hood pulled the bobbin and walked into her grandmother's cottage.

In the bed she saw someone wearing a shawl and nightcap. She was rather puzzled. Her grandmother seemed quite different. So she said,

"What big eyes you have, grandmother!"

"All the better to see you with!" said the wolf.

"What big ears you have, grandmother!"

"All the better to hear you with!" said the wolf.

"What big teeth you have, grandmother!"

"All the better to eat you with!" said the wolf and he sprang out of bed. He pounced on Little Red Riding Hood about to gobble her up.

Little Red Riding Hood screamed with fright. Luckily the woodcutters had just come out of the wood and were passing the cottage. They rushed inside and killed the wolf instantly. One of them then cut him open and out jumped the grandmother, who was feeling rather shaken by her adventure. However, she was delighted to see Little Red Riding Hood, who gave her the food she had brought in her basket and the bunch of flowers.

Little Red Riding Hood took care never to talk to wolves again, and she always stayed on the path whenever she went through the wood to visit her grandmother.

LION AT SCHOOL

Once upon a time there was a little girl who didn't like going to school. She always set off late. Then she had to hurry, but she never hurried fast enough.

One morning she was hurrying along as usual when she turned a corner and there stood a lion, blocking her way. He stood waiting for her. He stared at her with his yellow eyes. He growled, and when he growled the little girl could see that his teeth were as sharp as skewers and knives. He growled: "I'm going to eat you up."

"Oh, dear!" said the little girl, and she began to cry.

"Wait!" said the lion. "I haven't finished. I'm going to eat you up UNLESS you take me to school with you."

"Oh, dear!" said the little girl. "I couldn't do that. My teacher says we mustn't bring pets to school."

"I'm not a pet," said the lion. He growled again, and she saw that his tail swished from side to side in anger – *swish! swash! swish! swash!* "You can tell your teacher that I'm a friend who is coming to school with you," he said. "Now shall we go?"

The little girl had stopped crying. She said: "All right. But you must promise two things. First of all, you mustn't eat anyone: it's not allowed."

"I suppose I can growl?" said the lion.

"I suppose you can," said the little girl.

"And I suppose I can roar?"

"Must you?" said the little girl.

"Yes," said the lion.

"Then I suppose you can," said the little girl.

63

"And what's the second thing?" asked the lion.

"You must let me ride on your back to school."

"Very well," said the lion.

He crouched down on the pavement and the little girl climbed on his back. She held on by his mane. Then they went on together towards the school, the little girl riding the lion.

The lion ran with the little girl on his back to school. Even so, they were late. The little girl and the lion went into the classroom just as the teacher was calling the register.

The teacher stopped calling the register when she saw the little girl and the lion. She stared at the lion, and all the other children stared at the lion, wondering what the teacher was going to say. The teacher said to the little girl: "You know you are not allowed to bring pets to school."

The lion began to swish his tail – *swish! swash!* The little girl said quickly: "This is not a pet. This is my friend who is coming to school with me."

The teacher still stared at the lion, but she said to the little girl: "What is his name then?"

"Noil," said the little girl. "His name is Noil. Just Noil." She knew it would be no good to tell the teacher that her friend was a lion, so she had turned his name backwards: LION — NOIL.

The teacher wrote the name down in the register: NOIL. Then she finished calling the register.

"Betty Small," she said.

"Yes," said the little girl.

"Noil," said the teacher.

"Yes," said the lion. He mumbled, opening his mouth as little as possible, so that the teacher should not see his teeth as sharp as skewers and knives. He did not swish his tail. He did not growl. He sat next to the little girl as good as gold.

All that morning the lion sat up on his chair next to the little girl, like a big cat, with his tail curled round his front paws, as good as gold. No one saw his teeth, no one saw his claws. He didn't speak unless the teacher spoke to him. He didn't growl, he didn't roar.

At playtime the little girl showed the lion how to drink milk through a straw. "This is milk," she said. "It makes your teeth grow strong."

"Good," said the lion. "I want my teeth to be strong to crunch bones."

He finished his milk up.

They went into the playground. All the children stopped playing to stare at the lion. Then they went on playing again. The little girl stood in a corner of the playground, with the lion beside her.

"Why don't we play like the others?" the lion asked.

The little girl said, "I don't like playing because some of the big boys are so big and rough. They knock you over without meaning to."

The lion growled. "They wouldn't knock ME over," he said.

"There's one big boy – the very biggest," said the little girl. "His name is Jack Tall. He knocks me over on purpose."

"Which is he?" said the lion. "Point him out to me."

The little girl pointed out Jack Tall to the lion.

"Ah!" said the lion. "So that's Jack Tall."

Just then the bell rang again, and all the children went back to their classrooms. The lion went with the little girl and sat beside her while the teacher read a story aloud.

Then the children drew and wrote until dinnertime. The lion was hungry, so he wanted to draw a picture of his dinner.

"What will it be for dinner?" he asked the little girl. "I hope it's meat."

"No," said the little girl. "It will be fish fingers because today is Friday."

Then the little girl showed the lion how to hold the yellow crayon in his paw and draw fish fingers. Underneath his picture she wrote: "I like meat better than fish fingers."

Then it was dinnertime. The lion sat up on his chair at the dinner-table next to the little girl. There were fish fingers for dinner, with peas and mashed potatoes. Afterwards there was cake and custard. The lion ate everything on his plate, and then he ate anything that the little girl had left on her plate. He ate very fast and at the end he said: "I'm still hungry; I wish it had been meat."

After dinner the children went into the playground.

All the big boys were running about, and the very biggest boy, Jack Tall, came running towards the little girl. He was running in circles, closer and closer to the little girl.

"Go away," said the lion. "You might knock my friend over. Go away."

"Shan't," said Jack Tall. The little girl got behind the lion.

The lion began to swish his tail: *swish! swash!*

Jack Tall was running closer and closer and closer.

The lion growled. Then Jack Tall saw the lion's teeth as sharp as skewers and knives. He stopped running. He stood still. He stared.

The lion opened his mouth wider – so wide that Jack Tall could see his throat, opened wide and deep and dark like a tunnel to go into. Jack Tall went pale.

Then the lion roared.

He roared and he ROARED and he ROARED.

All the teachers came running out, to see what the matter was.

All the children stopped playing and stuck their fingers in their ears. And the biggest boy, Jack Tall, turned round and ran and ran and ran – out of the playground – out through the school gates – along the streets. He never stopped running until he got home to his mother.

The little girl came out from behind the lion. "Well," she said, "I don't think much of *him*. I shall never be scared of *him* again."

"I was hungry," said the lion, "I could easily have eaten him. Only I'd promised you."

"And his mother wouldn't have liked it," said the little girl. "Time for afternoon school now."

"I'm not staying for afternoon school," said the lion.

"See you on Monday then," said the little girl. But the lion did not answer. He just walked off.

On Monday morning the little girl started in good time for school, because she was looking forward to it. She arrived in good time, too.

She did not see the lion.

In the classroom the teacher called the register.

She came to the little girl's name.

"Betty Small," she said.

"Yes," said the little girl.

"Noil," said the teacher.

No one answered.

Later on, in the playground, the biggest boy came up to the little girl.

"Where's your friend that talks so loudly?" he said.

"He's not here today," said the little girl.

"Might he come another day?" asked the biggest boy.

"He might," said the little girl. "He easily might. So you just watch out, Jack Tall."

TEENY-TINY

There was once a teeny-tiny woman who lived in a teeny-tiny house in a teeny-tiny village.

One day this teeny-tiny woman put on her teeny-tiny bonnet, and went out of her teeny-tiny house to take a teeny-tiny walk. And when this teeny-tiny woman had gone a teeny-tiny way she came to a teeny-tiny gate; so the teeny-tiny woman opened the teeny-tiny gate, and went into a teeny-tiny churchyard. And when this teeny-tiny woman had got into the teeny-tiny churchyard, she saw a teeny-tiny bone on a teeny-tiny grave, and the teeny-tiny woman said to her teeny-tiny self, "This teeny-tiny bone will make me some teeny-tiny soup for my teeny-tiny supper." So the teeny-tiny woman put the teeny-tiny bone into her teeny-tiny pocket, and went home to her teeny-tiny house.

Now when the teeny-tiny woman got home to her teeny-tiny house she was a teeny-tiny bit tired; so she went up her teeny-tiny stairs to her teeny-tiny bed, and put the teen-tiny bone into a teeny-tiny cupboard. And when this teeny-tiny woman had been to sleep a teeny-tiny time, she was awakened by a teeny-tiny voice from the teeny-tiny cupboard, which said:

"Give me my bone!"

And this teeny-tiny woman was a teeny-tiny bit frightened, so she hid her teeny-tiny head under the teeny-tiny clothes and went to sleep again. And when she had been to sleep again a teeny-tiny time, the teeny-tiny voice again cried out from the teeny-tiny cupboard a teeny-tiny bit louder.

"Give me my bone!"

This made the teeny-tiny woman a teeny-tiny more frightened, so she hid her teeny-tiny head a teeny-tiny further under the teeny-tiny clothes. And when the teeny-tiny woman had been to sleep again a teeny-tiny time, the teeny-tiny voice from the teeny-tiny cupboard said again a teeny-tiny bit louder,

"Give me my bone!"

And this teeny-tiny woman was a teeny-tiny bit more frightened, but she put her teeny-tiny head out of the teeny-tiny clothes, and said in her loudest teeny-tiny voice, **"take it!"**

RAPUNZEL

A long time ago, a husband and wife lived happily in a cottage at the edge of a wood. But one day the wife fell ill. She could eat nothing and grew thinner and thinner. The only thing that could cure her, she believed, was a strange herb that grew in the beautiful garden next to their cottage. She begged her husband to find a way into the garden and steal some of this herb, which was called rapunzel.

Now this garden belonged to a wicked witch, who used it to grow herbs for her spells. One day, she caught the husband creeping into her garden. When he told her what he had come for, the witch gave him some rapunzel, but she made him promise to give her their first-born child in return. The husband agreed, thinking that the witch would soon forget the promise. He took the rapunzel back to his wife, who felt better as soon as she had eaten it.

A year later, a baby girl was born and the witch *did* come and take her away. She told the couple they would be able to see their daughter in the garden behind their house. Over the years they were able to watch her grow up into a beautiful child, with long fair hair. The witch called her Rapunzel after the plant her father had come to take.

When she was twelve years old, the witch decided to lock Rapunzel up in a high tower in case she tried to run away. The tower had no door or staircase, but Rapunzel was quite happy up there as she could sit at the window

71

watching the life of the forest and talking to the birds. Yet sometimes she would sigh, for she longed to be back in the beautiful garden where she could run and skip in the sunshine. Then she would sing to cheer herself up.

Each day, the witch came to see her, bringing fresh food. She would stand at the bottom of the tower and call out,

"Rapunzel, Rapunzel, let down your long hair."

Rapunzel, whose long golden hair was plaited, would twist it round one of the bars and drop it out of the window, and the witch would climb up it. When she left, Rapunzel would let down her golden hair again, and the witch would slide nimbly down to the ground.

One day, the king's son was riding through the forest when he heard Rapunzel singing. Mystified, he rode to the tower, but could see no door, so could not understand how anyone could be there. He decided to stay and watch the tower and listen to the singing. After a while the witch came along and the prince watched her carefully. To his amazement, as she called out,

"Rapunzel, Rapunzel, let down your long hair," a long golden plait of hair fell almost to the ground.

The prince saw the witch climb up the hair and disappear through the window, and he made up his mind he would wait until she had gone and see if he could do the same.

So after the witch had gone, he stood where the witch had been and called,

"Rapunzel, Rapunzel, let down your long hair."

When the golden plait came tumbling down, he climbed up as the witch had done and found to his astonishment the most beautiful girl he had ever seen. They talked for a long time and then the prince left, promising to come again. Rapunzel looked forward to his visits, for she had been lonely. He told her all about the world outside her tower, and they fell deeply in love.

One day Rapunzel said to the witch, "Why is it when you climb up my hair you are so heavy? The handsome prince who comes is much lighter than you." At this, the witch flew into a rage and took Rapunzel out of the tower and led her deep into the forest to a lonely spot, and told her she must stay there without food or shelter. The witch cut off Rapunzel's hair and then hurried back to the tower with the long plait of golden hair.

That evening when the prince came by, he called out as usual,

"Rapunzel, Rapunzel, let down your long hair."

The witch, who had secured the plait of golden hair inside the window, threw it down. The prince climbed up eagerly, only to be confronted with the wicked witch. "Aha," she cackled, "so you are the visitor who has been coming to see my little Rapunzel. I will make sure you won't see her again," and she tried to scratch out his eyes.

The prince jumped out of the high window, but was not killed for he landed in a clump of thorny bushes. His face, however, was badly scratched and his eyes hurt so that he could not see, and he stumbled off blindly into the forest.

After several days of wandering and suffering, he heard a voice singing. Following the sound, he drew closer and realized he had found Rapunzel, who was singing as she worked to make a home for herself in the forest. He ran towards her, calling her name, and she came and kissed him. As she did so, his eyes were healed and he could see again.

The prince took Rapunzel to his father's palace, where he told his story. Rapunzel was reunited with her parents who were overjoyed to see their daughter again, and a proclamation was made banning the witch from the kingdom. Then a grand wedding took place. Rapunzel married the prince and lived with him for many years. As for the witch, she was never seen again.

BEAUTY AND THE BEAST

A rich merchant who had three sons and three daughters lived in a big house in the city. His youngest daughter was so beautiful she was called Beauty by all who knew her. She was as sweet and good as she was beautiful. Sadly all of the merchant's ships were lost at sea and he and his family had to move to a small cottage in the country. His sons worked hard on the land and Beauty was happy working in the house, but his two elder daughters complained and grumbled all day long, especially about Beauty.

One day news came that a ship had arrived which would make the merchant wealthy again. The merchant set off to the city, and just before he left he said, "Tell me, daughters, what gifts would you like me to bring back for you?"

The two older girls asked for fine clothes and jewels, but Beauty wanted nothing. Realizing this made her sisters look greedy, she thought it best to ask for something. "Bring me a rose, father," she said, "just a beautiful red rose."

When the merchant reached the city he found disaster had struck once more and the ship's cargo was ruined. He took the road home wondering how to break the news to his children. He was so deep in thought that he lost his way. Worse still, it started to snow, and he feared he would never reach home alive. Just as he despaired he noticed lights ahead, and riding towards them he saw a fine castle. The gates stood open and flares were alight in the courtyard. In the stables a stall stood empty with hay in the manger and clean bedding on the floor ready for his horse.

The castle itself seemed to be deserted, but a fire was burning in the dining-hall where a table was laid with food. The merchant ate well, and still finding no one went upstairs to a bedroom which had been prepared. "It is almost as if I were expected," he thought.

In the morning he found clean clothes had been laid out for him and breakfast was on the table in the dining-hall. After he had eaten he fetched his horse and as he rode away he saw a spray of red roses growing from a rose bush. Remembering Beauty's request, and thinking he would be able to bring a present for at least one daughter, he plucked a rose from the bush.

Suddenly a beast-like monster appeared. "Is this how you repay my hospitality?" it roared. "You eat my food, sleep in my guest-room and then insult me by stealing my flowers. You shall die for this."

The merchant pleaded for his life, and begged to see his children once more before he died. At last the beast relented.

"I will spare your life," it said, "if one of your daughters will come here willingly and die for you. Otherwise you must promise to return within three months and die yourself."

The merchant agreed to return and went on his way. At home his children listened with sorrow to his tales of the lost cargo and his promise to the monster. His two elder daughters turned on Beauty, saying, "Your stupid request for a rose has brought all this trouble on us. It is your fault that father must die."

When the three months were up Beauty insisted on going to the castle with her father, pretending only to ride with him for company on the journey. The beast met them, and asked Beauty if she had come of her own accord, and she told him she had.

"Good," he said. "Now your father can go home and you will stay with me."

"What shall I call you?" she asked bravely.

"You may call me Beast," he replied.

Certainly he was very ugly and it seemed a good name for him. Beauty waved a sad farewell to her father. But she was happy that at least she had saved his life.

As Beauty wandered through the castle she found many lovely rooms and beautiful courtyards with gardens. At last she came to a room which was surely meant just for her. It had many of her favourite books and objects in it. On the wall hung a beautiful mirror and to her surprise, as she looked into it, she saw her father arriving back at their home and her brothers and sisters greeting him. The picture only lasted a few seconds then faded. "This Beast may be ugly, but he is certainly kind," she thought. "He gives me all the things I like and allows me to know how my family is without me."

That night at supper the Beast joined her at the candle-lit table. He sat and stared at her. At the end of

the meal he asked: "Will you marry me?"

Beauty was startled by the question but said as gently as she could, "No, Beast, you are kind but I cannot marry you."

Each day it was the same. Beauty had everything she wanted during the day and each evening the Beast asked her to marry him, and she always said no.

One night Beauty dreamt that her father lay sick. She asked the Beast if she could go to him, and he refused, saying that if she left him he would die of loneliness. But when he saw how unhappy Beauty was, he said:

"If you go to your family, will you return within a week?"

"Of course," Beauty replied.

"Very well, just place this ring on your dressing table the night you wish to return, and you shall come back

here. But do not stay away longer than a week, or I shall die."

The next morning Beauty awoke to find herself in her own home. Her father was indeed sick, but Beauty nursed him lovingly. Beauty's sisters were jealous once more. They thought that if she stayed at home longer than a week the Beast would kill her. So they pretended to love her and told her how much they had missed her. Before Beauty knew what had happened ten days had passed. Then she had a dream that the Beast was lying still as though he were dead by the lake near his castle.

"I must return at once," she cried and she placed her ring on the dressing table.

The next morning she found herself once more in the Beast's castle. All that day she expected to see him, but he never came. "I have killed the Beast," she cried, "I have killed him." Then she remembered that in her dream he had been by the lake and quickly she ran there. He lay still as death, down by the water's edge.

"Oh, Beast!" she wept, "Oh, Beast! I did not mean to stay away so long. Please do not die. Please come back to me. You are so good and kind." She knelt and kissed his ugly head.

Suddenly no Beast was there, but a handsome prince stood before her. "Beauty, my dear one," he said. "I was bewitched by a spell that could only be broken when a beautiful girl loved me and wanted me in spite of my ugliness. When you kissed me just now you broke the enchantment."

Beauty rode with the prince to her father's house and then they all went together to the prince's kingdom. There he and Beauty were married. In time they became king and queen, and ruled for many happy years.

MOTHER HOLLE

There was once a woman who had two daughters. One of them was pretty and worked hard and the other was ugly and lazy. Strange to say, the mother loved the lazy girl and she made the other one do all the work.

Each day when the housework was finished, she sent the pretty girl to sit by the well and spin some thread. This made the girl's fingers bleed and some drops of blood fell on the spindle. She bent over the well to wash it off and somehow the spindle fell into the water. She ran home in tears but her mother scolded her. "You dropped the spindle into the well, so you must get it out!"

The poor girl went outside. How could she find the spindle? In the end, she jumped into the well. All at once she found herself in a warm sunny meadow filled with flowers. Soon she noticed a lovely smell coming from a baker's oven filled with bread.

"Take us out! Take us out or we'll be burned! We were baked through, long ago!" the loaves cried. So she took them out and put them on the grass to cool.

She walked on until she came to an apple-tree full of apples.

"Shake me! Shake me, for my apples are ripe!" the tree cried. So she shook the tree until not a single apple was left. She heaped them neatly together before she walked away.

Next she saw a little house with an old woman standing outside. She had such large teeth that the girl was frightened.

"Don't run away, my child," she said, "if you will work in my house I will look after you. But you must be careful when you make my bed. You must shake the feathers very hard so that people on earth will say: 'Mother Holle must be making her bed for it is snowing today.'"

She spoke so kindly that the girl went inside the house and she did everything Mother Holle asked her to do. Whenever she turned the mattress over, the feathers danced like snowflakes. The old woman gave her wonderful food and never scolded or shouted at her.

She liked staying with Mother Holle, but in a little while she felt unhappy and realized that she wanted to go home. "Mother Holle," she said, "it is much nicer here than at home as my mother and sister are not at all kind to me. I've been very happy with you but they are my family so I must go back to see them."

"I am pleased that you want to see them," Mother Holle replied, "and as you have worked so well, I will take you home myself."

She took the girl to a big gate. "Go through there, my dear," she said and as it opened a shower of gold coins fell and the girl caught them in her apron.

"That is your reward for working hard and here is the spindle you dropped in the well," the old woman said.

The gate clanged shut and the girl found herself outside her house. The cock standing on the wall crowed:

> *"Cock-a-doodle-doo!*
> *Your golden daughter's come back to you!"*

She went inside and her mother and sister gasped enviously when they saw all the gold coins.

"How happy I am to see you," the mother said.

"I've missed you very much," said her sister untruthfully. They wanted to get their hands on the gold!

"How did you get that gold?" inquired her mother.

So her daughter told them what had happened.

"You can go and try your fortune, dear daughter," her mother said to the lazy girl, "you are just as clever, so just remember what you have to do."

So the girl took a spindle outside and sat by the well as her sister had done. She pricked her finger on a thorn and then squeezed a few drops of blood on the spindle. Then she threw it into the well and jumped in herself. Like her sister, she found herself in a beautiful meadow. She rushed straight across the meadow to the baker's oven filled with bread.

"Take us out! Take us out or we'll be burned! We were baked through long ago!" cried the loaves.

"Do you think I want to get hot and make my hands dirty pulling you out?" the lazy girl said and she walked on. Soon she reached the apple tree.

"Shake me! Shake me, for my apples are ripe!" the tree cried.

"Your apples are heavy and they might fall on my head and hurt me," she said and she walked away.

In a short time she saw Mother Holle's house. "I shan't be frightened of her large teeth," she thought, "for my sister warned me about them." She knocked and when the old woman came to the door she said:

"I've come to work for you," and she walked inside.

On the first day she worked hard. She did whatever Mother Holle asked, for she was hoping to get plenty of gold. The next day she did not work very well and on the third day she was so slow that she did not finish one single thing. Then she began to stay in bed in the mornings and soon she would not get up at all! Worst of all, she would not shake up the old woman's mattress properly so the feathers did not fly about and no snow fell over the earth.

At last Mother Holle told the lazy girl to go home. She was delighted. "I'll get the gold now," she thought. Mother Holle took her to the same gate she had opened for the other girl.

But when this girl went through, instead of gold, a big bucket of tar came pouring down.

"That is your reward!" Mother Holle said.

The lazy girl arrived home and the cock crowed:

> *"Cock-a-doodle-doo!*
> *Your dirty daughter's come back to you!"*

She could not wash away the tar, neither could her mother and it stuck to her for the rest of her life.

THESEUS AND THE MINOTAUR

Theseus is one of the great heroes of Greek legends and there are many stories told of his courage and his brave deeds. He was the son of Aegeus, King of Athens, whose country had been defeated in war by the Cretans, led by King Minos.

After the war, King Aegeus signed a treaty, promising that he would send to the island of Crete seven youths and seven maidens, who would be thrown into the labyrinth under the king's palace. A monster called the Minotaur lived in the labyrinth and it would kill the youths and maidens or else they would die from starvation. Each year there was great grief and sorrow when the seven young men and women were chosen and sent off to Crete.

Theseus was determined to stop this cruel sacrifice. Like everyone else, he hated to think of so many fine young people going off to their death every year. As soon as he was old enough, he insisted on going in place of one of the young men chosen.

The people did their best to stop him, saying that the king's son was needed by his people and that he would never return. His father, the king, pleaded with him until the moment when the boat was ready to sail. Then when he saw nothing could stop Theseus from going, he asked his son to promise one thing.

"If by some miracle you return, Theseus, change these black sails of mourning that are on the ship now to white sails. Every day I shall stand on the cliffs and watch for the ship's return. If the sails are white, I shall come to meet you. If they are black, I will throw myself off the cliffs down to the grey rocks and the sea below. For if you are dead I cannot live any longer."

Theseus promised that if he returned alive the black sails would be changed to white, and so, at last, the ship set sail.

When they arrived in Crete, Theseus asked to see King Minos, and when he was taken before the king he requested that he alone might go to the Minotaur, and that the other Athenians be set free at once. But King Minos refused. Theseus then asked to visit the Minotaur first. If he came away alive then his fellow countrymen should be returned to Athens. Minos agreed to this for he was sure that no one could ever come out of the labyrinth alive. He ordered that Theseus be taken to the labyrinth alone the very next evening.

Now King Minos had a daughter called Ariadne and she listened closely to Theseus as he talked to her father. She fell in love with the young prince and decided to help him. That night Ariadne came in disguise to the prison where the young Athenians were held, and spoke to Theseus. She told him that the Minotaur lived in a cavern at the centre of the labyrinth. She feared that Theseus would never find his way out of the labyrinth, for there were countless twists and turns in the passages and hundreds of choices of ways to go. It would be impossible to remember the way out even if he did fight and kill the Minotaur.

"Take this with you," said Ariadne, pressing into Theseus's hand a tiny ball of silken thread. "Let it unwind as you make your way into the labyrinth, and then if you do kill the Minotaur, you will be able to find your way out and escape before my father's guards kill you. When you are out of the labyrinth come down to the bay where your ship will be waiting."

"Who are you?" asked Theseus, "and why are you helping me in this way?"

"I am Ariadne, King Minos's daughter," she replied, "and I have heard many tales of your bravery, Theseus. If you escape the labyrinth I want you to take me away with you, for I am unhappy living here in Crete."

The next evening, the guards came to take Theseus to the Minotaur. They did not notice the knife that Theseus had concealed, nor the ball of silken thread which he started to unwind as soon as the guards left him at the entrance to the labyrinth.

Theseus wandered first down one passage, then down another, and another, and another, until he came at last to a large cavern at the centre of the labyrinth. There he paused on hearing a roaring bellowing sound. He tried to accustom his eyes to the dim light so that he could see what his opponent looked like. He had heard fearful stories about the Minotaur but no one had ever been able to describe it. Now, through the gloom, he saw a monstrous figure, half bull, half man. The creature sniffed the air as it smelt the stranger, then with a further bellow of rage, it thundered towards Theseus.

Theseus braced himself for the shock of the monster's charge. He was renowned for his strength and courage and at this moment, he badly needed both. He seized the bull's horns on the Minotaur's head as it charged towards him and he jumped neatly over its back. Again and again the Minotaur came at him, and again and again Theseus turned in time, using all his might to twist the thick neck each time he held the horns. The creature's strength gradually faded as Theseus, the champion wrestler of Athens, landed on his feet first on one side, then the other.

The blood was pounding in Theseus's head and his body ached. At last he twisted the monster's neck one more time as he jumped, and the Minotaur crashed to the ground, gasping.

Theseus quickly pulled the knife from its sheath and plunged it into the Minotaur's heart. He groped for Ariadne's thread at the entrance to the cavern and, keeping his hand on it, he followed it through the labyrinth until he reached the entrance. From there, by the light of the moon, he made his way down to the bay where he found his ship. Ariadne had forced her father's guards to release the other Athenians from prison, and as he climbed on board, the order was given to sail. They knew they must get away from Crete as quickly as possible as King Minos would be swift to avenge the death of the Minotaur.

Theseus found Ariadne waiting on the ship and he was glad to see her there for she was very beautiful. Moreover, now the Minotaur was dead, he had time to think of other things and it was not long before he fell in love with her. The ship sailed to another island called Naxos, where they disembarked and celebrated Theseus's great victory. They feasted and drank wine on Naxos for many days.

At last Theseus decided the time had come to return to Athens and tell his father that the Minotaur was dead and his people need no longer sacrifice seven youths and maidens each year. But Ariadne was happy on the island of Naxos and decided not to leave with Theseus and the other Athenians. So much had happened since leaving Athens that Theseus quite forgot his promise to his father and the ship sailed towards Athens still carrying black sails.

Each day, King Aegeus watched from the cliffs for his son. One morning, he saw the ship on which Theseus had left sail into sight. When he saw the black sails, the old king was overcome with grief at the thought of his son's death. Full of sorrow that he had allowed his son to go to Crete, he threw himself off the cliff down to the sharp grey rocks and churning sea below. To this day that part of the sea is called the Aegean Sea in his honour.

As for Theseus, he came home to a royal funeral, and not to the joyful celebrations he had planned.

TITTY MOUSE AND TATTY MOUSE

Titty Mouse and Tatty Mouse both lived in a house. Titty Mouse went gathering corn and Tatty Mouse went gathering corn, so they both went gathering corn.

Titty Mouse made a pudding, and Tatty Mouse made a pudding, so they both made a pudding. And Tatty Mouse put her pudding into the pot to boil, but when Titty went to put hers in, the pot tumbled over, and scalded her to death.

Then Tatty Mouse sat down and wept. A three-legged stool said, "Tatty, why do you weep?"

"Titty's dead," said Tatty, "and so I weep."

"Then," said the stool, "I'll hop." So the stool hopped.

Then a broom in the corner of the room said, "Stool, why do you hop?"

"Oh!" said the stool. "Titty's dead, and Tatty weeps, so I hop."

"Then," said the broom, "I'll sweep." So the broom began to sweep.

Then said the door, "Broom, why do you sweep?"

"Oh!" said the broom, "Titty's dead, and Tatty weeps, and the stool hops, and so I sweep."

"Then," said the door, "I'll jar." So the door jarred.

Then said the window, "Door, why do you jar?"

"Oh!" said the door, "Titty's dead, and Tatty weeps, and the stool hops, and the broom sweeps, and so I jar."

"Then," said the window, "I'll creak." So the window creaked.

Now there was an old bench outside the house, and when the window creaked, the bench said, "Window, why do you creak?"

"Oh!" said the window, "Titty's dead, and Tatty weeps, and the stool hops, and the broom sweeps, the door jars, and so I creak."

"Then," said the bench, "I'll run round the house." So the old bench ran round the house.

Now there was a fine large walnut tree growing by the cottage, and the tree said to the bench, "Bench, why do you run round the house?"

"Oh!" said the bench. "Titty's dead, and Tatty weeps, and the stool hops, and the broom sweeps, the door jars, and the window creaks, and so I run round the house."

"Then," said the walnut tree, "I'll shed my leaves." So the walnut tree shed all its beautiful leaves.

Now there was a little bird perched on one of the boughs of the tree, and when all the leaves fell, it said, "Walnut tree, why do you shed your leaves?"

"Oh!" said the tree, "Titty's dead, and Tatty weeps, the stool hops, and the broom sweeps, the door jars, and the window creaks, the old bench runs round the house, and so I shed my leaves."

"Then," said the little bird, "I'll moult all my feathers." So he moulted all his pretty feathers. Now there was a little girl walking below, carrying a jug of milk, and when she saw the poor bird moult all his feathers, she said, "Little bird, why do you moult all your feathers?"

"Oh!" said the little bird, "Titty's dead, and Tatty weeps, the stool hops, and the broom sweeps, the door jars, and the window creaks, the old bench runs round the house, the walnut tree sheds its leaves, and so I moult all

91

my feathers."

"Then," said the little girl, "I'll spill the milk." So she dropped the pitcher and spilt all the milk. Now there was an old man just by on the top of a ladder thatching a rick, and when he saw the little girl spill the milk, he said, "Little girl, why did you spill the milk?"

Then said the little girl, "Titty's dead, and Tatty weeps, the stool hops, and the broom sweeps, the door jars, and the window creaks, the old bench runs round the house, the walnut tree sheds its leaves, the little bird moults its feathers and so I spill the milk."

"Oh!" said the old man, "Then I'll tumble off the ladder and break my neck." So he tumbled off the ladder and broke his neck. And when the old man broke his neck, the great walnut tree fell down with a crash, and upset the old bench and house, and the house falling knocked the window out, and the window knocked the door down, and the door upset the broom, and the broom upset the stool, and poor Tatty Mouse was buried beneath the ruins.

GOLDILOCKS AND THE THREE BEARS

Once upon a time there were three bears who lived in a house in the forest. There was a great big father bear, a middle-sized mother bear and a tiny baby bear.

One morning, their breakfast porridge was too hot to eat, so they decided to go for a walk in the forest. While they were out, a little girl called Goldilocks came through the trees and found their house. She knocked on the door and, as there was no answer, she pushed it open and went inside.

In front of her was a table with three chairs, one large chair, one middle-sized chair and one small chair. On the table were three bowls of porridge, one large bowl, one middle-sized bowl and one small bowl – and three spoons.

Goldilocks was hungry and the porridge looked good, so she sat in the great big chair, picked up the large spoon and tried some of the porridge from the big bowl. But the chair was very big and very hard, the spoon was heavy and the porridge too hot.

Goldilocks jumped off quickly and went over to the middle-sized chair. But this chair was far too soft, and when she tried the porridge from the middle-sized bowl it was too cold. So she went over to the little chair and picked up the smallest spoon and tried some of the porridge from the tiny bowl.

This time it was neither too hot nor too cold. It was just right – and so delicious that she ate it all up. But she was too heavy for the little chair and it broke in pieces under her weight.

Next Goldilocks went upstairs, where she found three beds. There was a great big bed, a middle-sized bed and a tiny little bed. By now she was feeling rather tired, so she climbed into the big bed and lay down. The big bed was very hard and far too big. Then she tried the middle-sized bed, but that was far too soft, so she climbed into the tiny little bed. It was neither too hard nor too soft. In fact, it felt just right, all cosy and warm, and in no time at all Goldilocks fell fast asleep.

In a little while, the three bears came back from their walk in the forest. They saw at once that somebody had pushed open the door of their house and had been inside.

Father Bear looked around, then roared in a great big growly voice,

"SOMEBODY HAS BEEN SITTING IN MY CHAIR!"

Mother Bear said in a quiet gentle voice,

"Somebody has been sitting in my chair!"

Then Little Bear said in a small squeaky baby voice,

"Somebody has been sitting in my chair, and has broken it!"

Then Father Bear looked at his bowl of porridge and saw the spoon in it, and he said in his great big growly voice,

"SOMEBODY HAS BEEN EATING MY PORRIDGE!"

Then Mother Bear saw that her bowl had a spoon in it, and said in her quiet gentle voice,

"Somebody has been eating my porridge!"

Little Bear looked at his porridge bowl and said in his small squeaky baby voice,

"Somebody has been eating my porridge, and has eaten it all up!"

Then the three bears went upstairs, and Father Bear saw at once that his bed was untidy, and he said in his

great big growly voice,

"SOMEBODY HAS BEEN SLEEPING IN MY BED!"

Mother Bear saw that her bed, too, had the bed-clothes turned back, and she said in her quiet gentle voice,

"Somebody has been sleeping in my bed!"

Then Little Bear looked at his bed and said in his small squeaky baby voice,

"Somebody is sleeping in my bed, **now**!"

He squeaked so loudly that Goldilocks woke up with a start. She jumped out of bed, and away she ran, down the stairs and out into the forest. And the three bears never saw her again.

BRER RABBIT'S CHRISTMAS

Once upon a bright clear winter morning Brer Fox stole into Brer Rabbit's garden and dug up a big sackful of his best carrots. Brer Rabbit didn't see him as he was visiting his friend Brer Bear at the time. When he got home he was mighty angry to see his empty carrot-patch.

"Brer Fox! That's who's been here," cried Brer Rabbit, and his whiskers twitched furiously. "Here are his paw marks and some hairs from his tail. All my best winter carrots gone! I'll make him give them back or my name's not Brer Rabbit."

He went along, *lippity lip, clippity clip,* and his little nose wrinkled at the fragrant smell of soup coming from Brer Fox's house.

"Now see here," he called crossly. "I just know it's my carrots you're cooking. I want them back so you'd better open your door."

"Too bad," chuckled Brer Fox. "I'm not opening my door until winter is over. I have plenty of carrots thanks to my kind friend Brer Rabbit, and a stack of other food for Christmas as well. I'm keeping my windows shut and my door bolted, so do go away. I want to enjoy my first bowl of carrot soup in peace."

At this, Brer Rabbit kicked the door, *blim blam!* He hammered on the door, *bangety bang!* It wasn't any use. My, he was in a rage as he turned away. Kind friend Brer Rabbit indeed! He stomped off, muttering furiously. But soon he grew thoughtful, then he gave a hop or two

96

followed by a little dance. By the time he reached home he was in a mighty good temper. Brer Rabbit had a plan all worked out. He'd get his carrots back and annoy Brer Fox into the bargain!

On Christmas Eve, Brer Rabbit heaved a sack of stones on his shoulder and climbed up onto Brer Fox's roof. He clattered round the chimney making plenty of noise.

"Who's there?" Brer Fox called. "Go away at once. I'm cooking my supper."

"It's Father Christmas," replied Brer Rabbit in a gruff voice. "I've brought a sack full of presents for Brer Fox."

"Oh, that's different," said Brer Fox quickly. "You're most welcome. Come right along down the chimney."

"I can't. I'm stuck," Brer Rabbit said in his gruff Father Christmas voice. Brer Fox unbolted his door and went outside to take a look. Certainly he could see somebody on the roof so he rushed back inside and called,

"Well, Father Christmas, don't trouble to come down the chimney yourself. Just drop the sack of presents and I'll surely catch it."

"Can't. That's stuck too," yelled Brer Rabbit and he smiled to himself. "You'll have to climb up inside your chimney, Brer Fox, then catch hold of the piece of string around the sack and you can haul it down yourself."

"That's easy," Brer Fox cried, "here I come," and he disappeared up the chimney.

Like lightning, Brer Rabbit was off that roof and in through the open doorway. There were his carrots in a sack, and on the table was a fine cooked goose and a huge Christmas pudding. He grabbed them both, stuffed them into the sack and ran. *Chickle, chuckle,* how he did run.

That old Brer Fox struggled up the chimney, higher and higher. He couldn't see any string but he felt it hanging down so he gave a big tug. The sack opened and out tumbled all the stones, *clatter bang, bim bam,* right on Brer Fox's head. My, my, he certainly went down that chimney quickly. Poor Brer Fox! He'd lost his Christmas dinner and the carrots, and now he had a sore head.

That rascally Brer Rabbit laughed and laughed but he made sure he kept out of Brer Fox's way all that Christmas Day and for some time afterwards.

TOM THUMB

In King Arthur's palace there lived a wonderful magician called Merlin. He liked to dress like a beggar and travel round the country making people happy.

One day he was out on his travels and became very tired, so he called at a cottage to ask for food and shelter. The farmer and his wife invited him in and made him welcome. They were friendly but Merlin was sure they were unhappy so he asked:

"Is something troubling you, kind friends?"

"There are no children laughing happily here," said the man.

"Yes," added his wife, "how happy I'd be if we had a child – even if he were no bigger than the thumb on my husband's hand!"

Merlin smiled as he went on his way. Strange to say, the farmer's wife got her wish. She had a son who was strong, healthy and as long as his father's thumb! So they called him 'Tom Thumb'.

As Tom grew older, he was full of mischief and loved playing tricks. When he lost his marbles in games with other boys, he crept into their marble-bags, filled his pockets, then slipped out and joined the game again without being seen by anybody!

One day his mother was mixing a pudding. Tom climbed up to the edge of the bowl to take a look. Splish, splash! In he fell. His mother went on stirring and then she put the pudding in a hot dish. Tom's mouth was full of batter so he couldn't scream but he kicked and struggled so much that his mother thought the pudding was be-witched! She threw the dish outside and a poor tinker carried it away for his dinner.

By this time Tom had cleared his mouth and he shouted as loud as he could. The tinker was terrified. He threw the dish away and Tom wriggled free and crept home, covered with sticky batter.

His mother was very happy to see Tom again, as she had wondered where her son had got to. She washed him in a teacup of warm water and put him to bed.

Next day Tom's mother went to the meadow to milk the cow. She took him along and as it was quite windy, she tied him to a thistle so that he wouldn't blow away while she did the milking. The cow noticed the purple thistle and gulped it down in one mouthful, along with poor Tom! He was afraid that the cow's big teeth would chew him up.

"Mother, mother," he squeaked, "I'm in the cow's mouth!"

His mother dropped her milk-bucket and rushed to help. The cow was so surprised at the funny noises inside her mouth that she opened it wide – out popped Tom and his mother caught him in her apron. She carried him home, gave him a nice supper, then put him to bed.

Another day he went for a walk in the fields. His little legs soon grew tired and he stopped for a rest by some pretty flowers. Suddenly a raven swooped down, picked him up in its beak and carried him off, high into the sky. Tom was very scared but he pushed and kicked the raven's beak until it opened. Tom fell – straight into a deep river where a big fish swallowed him up at once.

Soon afterwards, a fisherman standing close by, caught the fish and took it to the market. He sold it to the

chief cook from the court of King Arthur who wanted to cook this fine fish for a royal feast.

The cook cut open the fish in the kitchen.

"Good gracious," she said, "whatever is this inside the fish! It looks like a toy." She held Tom Thumb up.

"Please ma-am," he piped, "I'm not a toy. I'm a b-b-boy. It was dark and scarey in there. Thank you very much for rescuing me."

Everybody in the kitchen crowded round to look at him. Then the cook carried him to King Arthur and put him on the King's Round Table. Tom bowed politely and the knights and their ladies clapped and bowed back. But Merlin the magician, who knew where Tom had come from, smiled quietly to himself.

Tom's funny tricks made King Arthur laugh and from then on he would pop Tom into his gold crown to carry him about.

One day King Arthur sent for Tom Thumb and asked:

"How big are your father and mother? Are they small like you?"

"No, your Majesty," said Tom, "my father is as tall as your knights and my mother is as tall as a queen. They are farmers and work hard to earn a living."

King Arthur carried Tom to his treasury where he kept his gold and silver. "There, Tom," he said, "take as much as you can carry, back home to your parents. But promise you will return within a month." Tom readily agreed and he chose a golden coin almost as big as himself.

"My parents can buy plenty of food now," he chuckled. He hoisted his coin on his back and, thanking King Arthur, set off for home. But it was hard work and Tom had to rest many times before he reached his father's house.

His mother cried with joy when she saw him.

"We thought we'd lost you forever," she said, "where have you been?"

"Down a furrow, up in the air, inside a fish!" Tom told them, "But the great King Arthur looked after me. Look, he sent this gold coin for you both."

They were grateful to the king and proud of Tom who was so tired with carrying the coin that he fell asleep curled up in a wooden spoon!

A month quickly passed by and Tom told his parents that he had promised to go back to King Arthur's court.

"We're sad to see you go, little son," they said.

"Please come back whenever you can."

King Arthur was happy to see him again and he ordered his own tailor to make Tom a wonderful purple velvet coat and cloak and breeches made of softest rabbit skin. The king ordered a tiny gold palace to be built and in the stable there was a tiny glass coach pulled by four white mice. Tom rode with the knights round the fields on a plump little mouse and he sat on the king's table in a tiny gold armchair. But Tom never forgot his father and mother. He often rode over to see them in his glass coach, which made them very happy. But they never knew that it was the magic of Merlin many years before, which had given them their wonderful son.

THE BIRDS' CONCERT

One morning when Bobby Brewster woke up he felt rather peculiar. First he shivered, and then he was far too hot and started to cough. When his mother heard him she came into his bedroom, had one look at his flushed face, and took his temperature. It was 102.

"Just you stay in bed and I'm going to send for the doctor," she said. So she did.

Dr Hopkins is a fat and jolly man and he came later in the morning. He looked at Bobby's throat, and tapped his chest, and made him say "Ah". "Have you got a tummy ache?" he asked.

"I'm afraid I have," said Bobby Brewster.

"Keep him in bed for a day or two. No rich food – like sardines – and send round to the chemist for this medicine."

So they did. And when Bobby took his first dose of medicine it tasted horrid.

He stayed in bed for two days, and by the next evening he felt a little better. Then, after he had been tucked in but before it was dark, he was lying listening to the birds saying, "Good evening", to each other, when a very funny thing happened. There was a tap-tap-tap on the windowsill. Bobby turned over, and there, standing on the windowsill, was a little bird. As soon as it saw that Bobby was looking, it winked – a great big wink with the left eye.

Of course Bobby winked back.

"Twitz – my friends in the winkers' club have asked

me to fly up and see how you are – twitz," said the bird.

"I'm a little better, thank you," said Bobby. "But still not quite well enough to get up."

"That's good – twitz –" said the bird. "We hope you will soon be quite well – twitz-twitz –"

"Thank you," said Bobby Brewster. "But what exactly do you mean by twitz?"

"I'm very sorry – twitz –" said the bird. "But I've got a nasty cough – twitz-twitz – and that's how birds cough – twitz –"

"Oh dear, I *am* sorry," said Bobby. "Are you taking anything for it?"

"I tried a bit of worm this morning, but it doesn't seem to have done much good," said the bird.

"Have you got a tummy ache?" asked Bobby.

"Yes, I'm afraid I have," said the bird.

"Do you know, I think you must have the same thing wrong with you as I have," said Bobby. "The doctor said, 'No rich food', so I shouldn't have any more worm if I were you."

"No, I don't intend to," said the bird.

Then Bobby Brewster had an idea.

"Why don't you try some of my medicine?" he said. "It's done me good so it might help you."

"What's it like?" asked the bird.

"Horrid," said Bobby. "But it's worth it if it makes you feel better."

"Very well. Thank you, I think I will," said the bird.

The medicine bottle was on Bobby's bedside table. He dipped in his little finger, and then held it over to the window. The bird hopped over and pecked at the drop of medicine on the end of his finger.

"Twitz-twitz," it said, and hopped up and down.

"Whatever's the matter?" cried Bobby.

"My word, you were quite right when you said the medicine was horrid," said the bird. "I've never tasted anything so nasty in my life – twitz – I *had* intended to sing you to sleep, but with this cough I should only sing out of tune and annoy you – twitz – If your medicine does me good I will come with my concert party tomorrow and give you a show. Would you like that?"

"It will be lovely," said Bobby – and the bird flew off, but it can't have lived far away because before he went to sleep Bobby could still hear the poor little thing twitz-twitzing in the trees.

The next morning at about seven o'clock Bobby opened a sleepy eye. Then a very funny thing happened. There was a tap-tap-tap-tap-tapping on the window. Not just a tap-tap-tap this time, but a long tap-tap-tap-

tap-tap. Bobby looked over, and there, standing on the windowsill, were seven birds. Bobby's friend, five other little birds like him – and a large fat black crow.

"Good morning, how do you feel?" asked the bird.

"I don't really know yet. I'm only just awake," said Bobby. "How are you?"

"I'm MUCH better," said the bird. "May I introduce you to Percy's Perkies?"

"Percy's Perkies?" said Bobby.

"Yes. I forgot to tell you last night that my name is Percy," said the bird. "And these are my Perkies."

"How do you do?" said Bobby, and the birds all bowed politely.

"Shall we start the show?" asked Percy.

"Whenever you like," said Bobby Brewster.

Well – you never saw such a show as those birds performed on Bobby Brewster's windowsill that morning. They had lovely voices – all except the crow – and they started with a song that Percy had specially written. This is how it went. (Sung to the tune of Boccerini's minuet.)

"Isn't it a pity Bobby's got a stomach ache?
Isn't it a pity Bobby's got a stomach ache?
Oh he felt so ill, he had to take a pill.
Bobby Brewster's got a stomach ache.
With fun – skawk-skawk-skwark.
And chaff – skwawk-skwawk-skwak.
We'll make – skawk-skwawk-skwawk.
Him laugh – skawwk-skwak-skwawk.
Sing a little song and he'll forget his stomach ache.
Won't be very long before he's lost his stomach ache.
With some fun and rhythm, that's the stuff to give 'em.
Bobby Brewster's got no stomach ache."

Of course, the little birds sung the words and the fat crow did the skwawks.

After that they did a clever little dance on one leg all together – all except the crow, that is. He tried to, but fell bonk on his back feather, which made Bobby laugh and he had to hide his face under the pillow to stop making too much noise.

But that wasn't all. After that they did a very clever juggling act with some peas that they must have pecked out of the pods in the garden. They threw them from beak to beak, and balanced them on their back feathers – all except the fat crow, that is – and he got a pea stuck so hard on his beak that he couldn't open his mouth. This made Bobby laugh so loudly that tears came into his eyes, the birds flew away, and Mrs Brewster came running into the bedroom.

"Whatever's the matter?" she cried. Then she looked at him more closely. "You look much better," she said.

"I AM much better," said Bobby Brewster. And when Dr Hopkins came later that morning he said that Bobby had made a remarkable recovery and the medicine must have done him a lot of good.

I suppose that's true in a way, because, after all, the medicine had cured Percy the bird as well. But I don't think Bobby would have got better quite so quickly if he hadn't seen the marvellous show given by Percy's Perkies on his windowsill that morning, do you?

Which all goes to show what a good thing it is to be a member of the winkers' club, doesn't it?

THE LION
AND THE MOUSE

A lion was lying asleep one day when a little mouse scampered over him, and woke him up. The lion put out his great big paw and trapped the mouse. He was just going to kill him when the mouse squeaked.

"I meant you no harm, Lion, please let me go free. If you do I promise I will help you one day."

"How can a mouse help a lion?" asked the lion scornfully. But he let the mouse go, and went back to sleep.

A little later the lion was caught in a trap laid by hunters. As he struggled, the ropes tightened around him and he lay on the ground exhausted. He knew that the hunters would soon come back and kill him.

Suddenly there was a rustling and the little mouse was beside him gnawing at the ropes. Strand by strand they broke as the mouse's sharp teeth worked away, and long before the hunters came back the lion was free.

"You never believed I could help you," said the mouse, "but even a mouse can help a lion, and one good turn deserves another."

A LION
IN THE MEADOW

The little boy said, "Mother, there is a lion in the meadow."

The mother said, "Nonsense, little boy."

The little boy said, "Mother, there is a big yellow lion in the meadow."

The mother said, "Nonsense, little boy."

The little boy said, "Mother, there is a big, roaring, yellow, whiskery lion in the meadow!"

The mother said, "Little boy, you are making up stories again. There is nothing in the meadow but grass and trees. Go into the meadow and see for yourself."

The little boy said, "Mother, I'm scared to go into the meadow, because of the lion which is there."

The mother said, "Little boy, you are making up stories – so I will make up a story too . . . Do you see this match box? Take it out into the meadow and open it. In it will be a tiny dragon. The tiny dragon will grow into a big dragon. It will chase the lion away."

The little boy took the match box and went away. The mother went on peeling the potatoes.

Suddenly the door opened.

In rushed a big, roaring, yellow, whiskery lion.

"Hide me!" it said. "A dragon is after me!"

The lion hid in the broom cupboard.

Then the little boy came running in.

"Mother," he said. "That dragon grew too big. There is no lion in the meadow now. There is a DRAGON in the meadow."

The little boy hid in the broom cupboard too.

"You should have left me alone," said the lion. "I eat only apples."

"But there wasn't a real dragon," said the mother. "It was just a story I made up."

"It turned out to be true after all," said the little boy. "You should have looked in the match box first."

"That is how it is," said the lion. "Some stories are true, and some aren't. But I have an idea. We will go and play in the meadow on the other side of the house. There is no dragon there."

"I am glad we are friends now," said the little boy.

The little boy and the big roaring, yellow, whiskery lion went to play in the other meadow. The dragon stayed where he was, and nobody minded.

The mother never ever made up a story again.

THE UGLY DUCKLING

One summer, when the corn was golden yellow and the hay was being dried in the fields, a mother duck was sitting on her nest of eggs. She sat in the rushes of a deep moat that surrounded a lovely country manor and waited for her eggs to hatch. It was taking a very long time and she was getting very tired.

At last one day she felt a movement beneath her. The eggs began to crack and out popped tiny fluffy ducklings. All the eggs hatched except for one, which was larger than the rest. The mother duck was impatient to take her new ducklings swimming but could not leave the last egg unhatched. She sat for a few more days, and just as she was about to give up, she heard a tapping and out of the shell tumbled the oddest ugliest duckling she had ever seen.

She took the babies into the water and proudly watched as they all swam straightaway, even the ugly duckling. She led them in a procession around the moat, showing them off to the other ducks. As they bobbed along behind her she heard many quacks of admiration and praise for her fine family. But she also heard laughter and scorn poured on the ugly duckling at the end of the line.

"He has been too long in the egg," she explained, "he has not come out quite the right shape. But he is strong and will grow into a fine duck soon."

As the weeks went by, and the corn was harvested in the fields, the ducklings grew up into ducks. But the ugly duckling with his grey feathers and clumsy shape remained different. All the ducks on the moat pecked him and made fun of him and refused to let him join in their games on the water.

At last the ugly duckling could bear it no more. As the autumn leaves began to fall he flew away to a great marsh. There he stayed alone, hiding from the ducks among the reeds.

One day he heard a strange cry and the sound of wings in the air. Looking up he saw three dazzling white birds flying majestically overhead. The ugly duckling felt a strange longing. He did not know the name of those birds but he felt he loved them more than he had loved anything before. He watched as they passed over his head and flew beyond until they were out of sight.

Autumn turned to winter, and the ugly duckling suffered many hardships.

The marshy water froze over with the cold weather and the poor duckling became trapped fast in the ice. A kind man happened to come by and he saw that he was in trouble. He broke the ice with his shoe and freed the duckling and carried him to his home. His children made a great fuss of the duckling and wanted to take hold of him. But the ugly duckling was frightened and flapped his wings in alarm. He upset a bucket of milk and fled as people ran after him shouting.

He struggled through many other difficulties during his first winter, but at last spring came, and with it warm sunshine. The ugly duckling felt better than he had done for months and flapped his wings. To his surprise they felt bigger and stronger, and he found he was flying easily away from the marsh towards a large and beautiful lake.

He alighted on the water and saw before him the three

wonderful birds he had seen flying overhead several months before. As the swans glided smoothly over the lake, the ugly duckling felt drawn to them, but he was sure they would peck and tease him like the ducks because he was so ugly.

At last he thought, "It's better to be hurt or even killed by birds as lovely as these than to be teased by those ducks," and he floated slowly towards them. "Kill me, kill me," he whispered as he drew nearer and he bent his neck in shame.

All at once he saw a reflection in the smooth lake waters. A beautiful swan with glossy white feathers and a fine yellow beak stared up at him. He moved; the swan moved. He opened his wings; so did the swan. The ugly duckling suddenly realized – he was a swan.

The other swans swam gracefully towards him, welcoming him and stroking him with their beaks. Some children came running down to the lake and called out to their father.

"Look a new swan has appeared. He is more beautiful than any of the others!" The children clapped their hands together in delight and they threw pieces of bread into the water for him.

The young and beautiful swan felt quite shy with all this attention, and hid his head under his wing. But, as the lilac trees bent their branches down to the water and the sun shone warm and bright, he felt a deep happiness. He rustled his feathers, arched his sleek long neck and said to himself, "I never dreamed of such great happiness when I was the Ugly Duckling."

TIM RABBIT'S MAGIC CLOAK

It was autumn, the beech leaves were falling from the great trees and covering the ground with a carpet of russet brown. Tim Rabbit came hurrying out of his house with a little old kite in his paws. It was a kite his father had made from willow twigs and a torn paper bag he had found on the common. It had a real string to hold it, but the tail was ragged.

"Good-bye, Mother," called Tim, "I may fly to the moon. Good-bye."

"Whatever do you mean?" asked Mrs Rabbit, following him to the doorway on the common. She looked up at the sky and saw the golden brown leaves drifting down and the pale young moon dimly shining.

"I'm going to fly my kite, Mother," said Tim again. "Good-bye."

Mrs Rabbit laughed and watched her son skip down the path and enter the wood. Then she went back to her house, but Tim trundled his soft little feet in the golden leaves, making a sweet sursurring sound, a rustle that fascinated him.

"All these leaves and plenty more on the trees," he thought. "I could make a tail for my kite and then I could make – yes, I could – a cloak for my mother."

He sat down and tossed the leaves in the air and then he drew a heap around him. He fastened a lot of leaves to the kite's bare tail, where the paper had torn away, and soon the kite was ready.

"Now for my mother's cloak," he muttered. He

searched in the gorse bushes for a good sharp needle, and he found some wisps of sheep's wool in the edge by the field. He 'teased' the wool between his paws to make a long thread, and he tied this to his needle of gorse. Then he began to stitch the leaves. He worked very hard, making long strings of leaves and joining them together, and he was so intent he did not notice that somebody was watching him. Each little leaf was sewn to another leaf until he had a large web of beech leaves with here and there a nut leaf or an oak leaf with an acorn.

He began to sing in a soft little voice, and somebody listened.

> *"Brown leaf, yellow leaf, red and gold,*
> *Striped leaf and speckled leaf, to keep out the cold.*
> *Good little Tim, to make a fine cloak,*
> *Mother will smile and think it's a joke.*
> *Then she will wear it and be a fine lady.*
> *To walk in the fields and woodland shady."*

He heard a little cough and he looked up quickly. Watching him was his cousin Sam Hare. "Oh, Sam. I didn't see you. I thought you were the fox," he cried.

"If I were a fox I could have eaten you," said Sam Hare.

"But you are only a hare," snorted Tim.

"What have you been making, Tim?" asked Sam.

"I've mended my kite and made a cloak for my mother's birthday, to keep her warm in cold weather," said Tim proudly and he held up the cloak with its brown-gold leaves.

"Oo-oo," said Sam. "How clever you are, Tim. I wish – I wish I were clever too."

"Never mind, Sam. I am, of course, no Ordinary Rabbit! You can fly my kite," said Tim.

They set off together, Tim holding the cloak and Sam dragging the kite. They left the wood and climbed a little hill. Tim laid the cloak on the ground with a stone on it to say it was private property, and Sam and he ran together holding the kite by its long string.

Sometimes it flopped and danced on the ground, and then it rose up and flew in the air, tugging at the string to get loose.

"Oh, Sam," cried Tim. "Suppose it lifted us both up in the air and took us to the moon."

They ran and ran, but the kite never rose very high, for the wind was half asleep. Suddenly Tim remembered his cloak. He hoped it was safe. So they turned round and ran with the kite to the little hill where they had started. There sat the fox, watching the cloak in a puzzled way.

"Hello, Tim Rabbit," said the fox, lazily stretching himself. "Is this your heap of leaves?"

"Yes – yes," stammered Tim, but Sam Hare hid behind a bush.

"What is it?" asked the fox.

"Only a heap of leaves, and yet it's a cloak for my mother," said Tim.

"A cloak?" echoed the fox.

"Yes, you wear it like this," said Tim eagerly, and he picked it up and flung it round his body, so that he was hidden in the folds of red and gold leaves.

"You are invisible," said the fox slowly.

"Yes," said Tim, and he started to run, holding the cloak tightly round him and clasping the kite string. The wind lifted the kite and caught the leafy cloak, carrying Tim off his feet. There he was in the air, with his little feet paddling, trying to find the ground.

"Oh, I say. I'm flying," he cried. "Oh. Oh."

"Dear me," said the fox. "How remarkable!" He leapt up but he could not reach Tim Rabbit.

Away flew Tim with the wind filling the leafy cloak and tugging at the kite.

"Poof! Poof!" shouted the wind. "Here's a fine cloud of beech leaves," and it tossed Tim up in the air and swept him far away.

"It's not beech leaves. It's me," cried Tim, but the wind did not hear as it strode through the sky.

Down below the fox stared, and then he went home. Little Sam Hare came out from behind the bush, and he scampered away to Tim's house.

"Mammy Rabbit!" he called knocking at the door.

"Your Tim has flown away. He's gone towards the moon, Mammy Rabbit."

Mrs Rabbit began to cry. She went out to the fields and she saw a tiny speck up in the sky. She was sure it was Tim, so she went home and sat down to cry even more.

Tim was enjoying himself as he floated along with the leafy cloak billowing around him, and the kite soaring above. He sang a little song which pleased the wind as it carried this small morsel high above the tree tops.

"Here I am, up in the sky,
Like a swallow, flying high,
Swept by the wind, held by the cloak,
Fluttering leaves, drifting like smoke."

Then Tim glanced down and saw in the distance the great blue sea and the little curling white waves. He felt very frightened and he sang again:

120

"Please Mr Wind, don't let me fall,
I'm only a rabbit, young and small.
Don't let me tumble down in the sea,
Do take me home to my mother for tea."

"A rabbit," said the wind. "Tim Rabbit." It swung round from north-east, to south, and swept little Tim Rabbit away from the sea.

It hovered for a few minutes over Tim's home and then gently dropped Tim, down, down, down, like a bundle of leaves and fur to the ground.

"Good-bye, Tim," cried the wind and it blew the trees and sent showers of leaves to fall over him.

Tim scrambled to his feet, still holding the kite's string. He ran to the house, kicked the door open and flung himself into his mother's arms.

"Oh, oh," cried Mrs Rabbit. "A bundle of leaves? No, it's Tim, my darling lost Tim. Where have you been, Tim? Sam Hare told me you had gone to the moon. And what's this you are wearing?"

"It's your birthday present, Mother," laughed Tim. "I made it for you. I made it myself out of a lot of leaves, and, Mother, if you wear it when the wind blows you can fly too."

"Oh, thank you, Tim," said Mrs Rabbit. "This is a lovely cloak. Red and gold and brown, and well sewn. I am proud to wear it. It will keep me warm in the snow."

She put the cloak round her shoulders and walked about the room with her usual dancing step.

"Brown leaf, yellow leaf, red leaf and gold,
Striped leaf, and speckled leaf to keep out the cold,"

sang Tim, dancing after her.

"Mother. You are just like a heap of leaves walking in the wind," said Tim. "Nobody can spy you. They will think you are only leaves, or maybe a little brown bush."

Mrs Rabbit threw off the cloak and laughed.

"Leaves walking," said the fox when a heap of golden leaves rolled past his den one day.

"Leaves talking," he muttered as he heard a tiny voice sing *"Brown leaf, yellow leaf, red and gold."*

"There's too much education these days. Leaves talking!" he added crossly. Wise Owl explained that it was a magical cloak, called by a grand name. It was a "Camoophlaged Cloak", to make something look like something else to save them from bad things.

"Cam-oo-phlaged cloak," sneezed the fox. "I should like a cam-oo-phlaged coat myself, striped yellow and brown."

"Ask Tim Rabbit to make it for you," said the owl. "He might, you know."

THE LITTLE FIR TREE

Anna pulled her boots on hard and stumped outdoors. "I don't want to go to school tomorrow!" she thought crossly. "I want it to be Christmas again. It's not fair . . . it went so fast, and now there's another whole year to wait!"

Suddenly something bright and golden caught her eye. In a corner of the garden stood the Christmas tree, where someone had thrown it on Twelfth Night, with its golden star still on the top.

"Oh good, I can have it for dressing up," she said, pulling the star off the prickly little tree. And then she said, "Poor tree, all bare and cold."

"Mmm . . ." sighed the tree; it was just green enough to speak still. "I'm a poor bare tree, thrown outside, and now my star's gone too, like everything else."

"Oh, don't be sad," said Anna kindly. "Think how pretty you were at Christmas, all sparkling and green."

"Yes," answered the tree, "I was very fine, wasn't I, all lit up day and night, with my coloured lights, and tiny toys, and shiny sweets and golden decorations? The children loved me, just like the sparrows said they would."

"Which sparrows?" asked Anna.

"The sparrows in the forest when I was one year old. I was green and alive and growing then, and I didn't realize how lucky I was to be at home with my family. The sparrows had been to the farmhouse nearby at Christmas time, and had peeped in at the windows. 'There's a fir tree in there,' they twittered excitedly, 'but you'd hardly recognize it. It's covered in tinsel, lights and little presents, and on the top there is a golden star. The children think it's the most beautiful tree in the whole world.' From that moment, I only wanted one thing: to be a Christmas tree. I couldn't wait to grow big enough. And I never took any notice of what the sun said to me!"

"The sun? What did the sun say?" asked Anna.

"'Gently now, little one,' he warned in his kind

smiling voice. 'You're still young; enjoy yourself while you can. Feel my warmth on your branches; feel the soft rain kissing your boughs, stretch and bend in the wind.' But all that just made me cross . . . who'd want to be stuck in a forest when they could be decorated and admired?"

"I've always wanted to go to a real forest," said Anna. "Didn't you like it there?"

"No, I didn't, because I was the smallest – even when I stretched – and children used to point at me and say what a dear little tree I was, and the hare used to jump right over me, just to make it worse. I couldn't wait to grow big like the others. Next year the woodman came and chose the tallest trees for ships' masts. How wonderful, I thought, they'll see the world. When shall I grow tall enough to be a mast and see the world?"

"But you never did, did you?" said Anna.

"No," whispered the forlorn tree, its voice dry and cracked, "I just waited impatiently there; waiting, waiting without seeing. The soft cold snow piled up on my branches; then the spring rain splashed down on me, and the sun warmed me. But I was just waiting for that woodman to come and choose me to be a Christmas tree, to be beautiful and admired. And do you know, the thrush chose me to hold her nest for her one spring. And I sheltered her little ones . . ."

"You were very lucky," said Anna.

"Yes I was, but all I could think of was Christmas, I couldn't wait for the woodman to choose me."

"And then what happened?" asked Anna, who was pressed right up close to the poor, prickly little brown tree so she could hear.

"And then," the poor tree sighed, "the woodman came at last, swinging his sharp axe. When he saw me, he said, 'There's a good one!' How proud I was, how excited, my dreams were coming true! Then he swung his axe, and felled me. How sudden it was, what cold cruel metal! I flung out my branches, but it was no use, and I crashed down hurt and dizzy." The tree was silent for a moment, and then went on more cheerfully.

"Next thing I knew I was in a warm room in a tub, and your mother was saying what a lovely tree I was. She hung me with shiny baubles that tickled my branches; and the lights, they were a bit hot, but so pretty. And then you came in with your friends, and you looked so pleased. I really bristled with pride because you all loved me so. And you danced and sang, and opened presents, and pulled the sweets off my branches: how tightly I was holding them!"

Anna put her arms round the little tree, who had once been so proud and green.

"So you did enjoy Christmas after all," she said.

"Yes, yes I did. But how soon it was over! How weak I felt afterwards, and then how homesick for my forest . . ." The tree's voice faded away.

Just then, a sharp wind blew the golden star right out of the little girl's hand, and made her shiver. And when Anna turned back to the little fir tree again, all its dry brown needles had fallen.

HOW THE POLAR BEAR BECAME

W hen the animals had been on earth for some time
they grew tired of admiring the trees, the flowers,
and the sun. They began to admire each other. Every
animal was eager to be admired, and spent a part of each
day making itself look more beautiful.

Soon they began to hold beauty contests.

Sometimes Tiger won the prize, sometimes Eagle,
and sometimes Ladybird. Every animal tried hard.

One animal in particular won the prize almost every
time. This was Polar Bear.

Polar Bear was white. Not quite snowy white, but
much whiter than any of the other creatures. Everyone
admired her. In secret, too, everyone was envious of her.
But however much they wished that she wasn't quite so

beautiful, they couldn't help giving her the prize.

"Polar Bear," they said, "with your white fur, you are almost too beautiful."

All this went to Polar Bear's head. In fact, she became vain. She was always washing and polishing her fur, trying to make it still whiter. After a while she was winning the prize every time. The only times any other creature got a chance to win was when it rained. On those days Polar Bear would say:

"I shall not go out into the wet. The other creatures will be muddy and my white fur may get splashed."

Then, perhaps, Frog or Duck would win for a change.

She had a crowd of young admirers who were always hanging around her cave. They were mainly Seals, all very giddy. Whenever she came out they made a loud shrieking roar:

"Ooooooh! How beautiful she is!"

Before long, her white fur was more important to Polar Bear than anything. Whenever a single speck of dust landed on the tip of one hair of it – she was furious.

"How can I be expected to keep beautiful in this country!" she cried then. "None of you have ever seen me at my best, because of the dirt here. I am really much whiter than any of you have ever seen me. I think I shall have to go into another country. A country where there is none of this dust. Which country would be best?"

She used to talk this way because then the Seals would cry:

"Oh, please don't leave us. Please don't take your beauty away from us. We will do anything for you."

And she loved to hear this.

Soon animals were coming from all over the world to look at her. They stared and stared as Polar Bear stretched out on her rock in the sun. Then they went off home and tried to make themselves look like her. But it was no use. They were all the wrong colour. They were black, or brown, or yellow, or ginger, or fawn, or speckled, but none of them was white. Soon most of them gave up trying to look beautiful. But they still came every day to gaze enviously at Polar Bear. Some brought picnics. They sat in a vast crowd among the trees in front of her cave.

"Just look at her," said Mother Hippo to her children. "Now see that you grow up like that."

But nothing pleased Polar Bear.

"The dust these crowds raise!" she sighed. "Why can't I ever get away from them? If only there were some spotless, shining country, all for me . . ."

Now pretty well all the creatures were tired of her being so much more admired than they were. But one creature more so than the rest. He was Peregrine Falcon.

He was a beautiful bird, all right. But he was not white. Time and time again, in the beauty contest he was runner-up to Polar Bear.

"If it were not for her," he raged to himself, "I should be first every time."

He thought and thought for a plan to get rid of her. How? How? How? At last he had it.

One day he went up to Polar Bear.

Now Peregrine Falcon had been to every country in the world. He was a great traveller, as all the creatures well knew.

"I know a country," he said to Polar Bear, "which is so clean it is even whiter than you are. Yes, yes, I know, you are beautifully white, but this country is even whiter. The rocks are clean glass and the earth is frozen ice-cream. There is no dirt there, no dust, no mud. You would

become whiter than ever in that country. And no one lives there. You could be queen of it.''

Polar Bear tried to hide her excitement.

"I could be queen of it, you say?" she cried. "This country sounds made for me. No crowds, no dirt? And the rocks, you say are glass?"

"The rocks," said Peregrine Falcon, "are mirrors."

"Wonderful," said Polar Bear.

"And the rain," he said, "is white face powder."

"Better than ever!" she cried. "How quickly can I be there, away from all these staring crowds and all this dirt?"

"I am going to another country," she told the other animals. "It is too dirty here to live."

Peregrine Falcon hired Whale to carry his passenger. He sat on Whale's forehead, calling out the directions. Polar Bear sat on the shoulder, gazing at the sea. The Seals, who had begged to go with her, sat on the tail.

After some days, they came to the North Pole, where it is all snow and ice.

"Here you are," cried Peregrine Falcon. "Everything

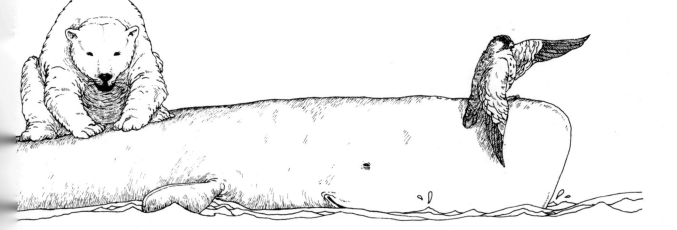

just as I said. No crowds, no dirt, nothing but beautiful clean whiteness."

"And the rocks actually are mirrors!" cried Polar Bear, and she ran to the nearest iceberg to repair her beauty after the long trip.

Every day now, she sat on one iceberg or another, making herself beautiful in the mirror of ice. Always, near her, sat the Seals. Her fur became whiter and whiter in this new clean country. And as it became whiter, the Seals praised her beauty more and more. When she herself saw the improvement in her looks she said:

"I shall never go back to that dirty old country again."

And there she still is, with all her admirers around her. Peregrine Falcon flew back to the other creatures and told them that Polar Bear had gone for ever. They were all very glad, and set about making themselves beautiful at once. Every single one was saying to himself:

"Now that Polar Bear is out of the way, perhaps I shall have a chance of the prize at the beauty contest."

And Peregrine Falcon was saying to himself:

"Surely, now, I am the most beautiful of all creatures."

But that first contest was won by a Little Brown Mouse for her pink feet.

LAZY JACK

There was once a boy called Jack who lived with his mother in a little cottage. His mother worked very hard but Jack sat by the fire in winter and stretched out on the grass when the sun shone. Everybody called him 'Lazy Jack'. One fine morning his mother said: "You must find some work if you want any more food in this house."

So on Monday Jack went to a farmer nearby and he worked in the fields for a penny. On the way home he felt tired for he was not used to doing any work, so he had a rest by a stream.

The penny he had earned jumped out of his hand and fell into deep water.

"Silly Jack," his mother said, when Jack told her what had happened. "Why didn't you put it in your pocket?"

"I'll do so next time," promised Jack.

On Wednesday Jack went to a dairy and the dairyman gave him a jar of creamy milk as his pay. Jack put the jar in his pocket. Well, every single drop of milk was spilt before he got home!

"Oh dear," said his mother, "you should have carried the jar on your head."

"I'll do so next time," said Jack.

He went back on Thursday to the farmer, who promised to give him a big cream cheese for working in his fields. Jack took it and put it carefully on his head.

It was a warm evening and on reaching home the cheese had melted and was stuck to his hair.

"You stupid boy!" his mother cried. "Why ever didn't you carry it carefully in your hands?"

"I'll do so next time," came Jack's reply.

On Friday Jack went to work for a baker for the day. He said he would give Jack a beautiful cat as his pay. Jack lifted up the cat and held it in his hands. But when he was walking home the cat scratched his arms so badly that Jack let it go and it ran happily back to the baker.

"You are silly," his mother said when he told her his sad story. "You should have tied a string to pussy and pulled him along behind you!"

"I'll do so next time," said Jack.

On Saturday Jack did some work for the butcher who gave him a fine big leg of lamb to take home. Jack was very pleased. He took out some string and tied it round the meat. Then he trailed it behind him all the way home.

It was ruined! Dust, stones and pieces of grass covered the meat. Jack's mother was angry. "I wanted to cook that meat for Sunday dinner!" she shouted. "Now we'll have to make do with cabbage. You should have carried it on your shoulders."

"I'll do so next time," said Jack once again.

When Monday came, Jack went out and this time he worked for a cattle-seller. He gave Jack a fine donkey at the end of the day. It was very lively and very heavy and Jack had a terrible time getting that donkey on his shoulders! At last he managed to hoist it up but it wasn't easy to keep it there. Jack walked slowly home with the donkey braying "Ee-aw, ee-aw, ee-aw" all the time. People smiled as they passed him, but Jack did not notice them for it was such hard work holding onto the donkey.

On the way he came up to a big house where a rich man lived with his beautiful daughter. Sad to say, she never said a word to anyone. She had never laughed either and the doctors told her father that she would never speak until somebody made her laugh for the first time.

On this day, the beautiful girl was standing by the window and was looking out when Jack came struggling past with the donkey across his shoulders. Its legs were sticking straight up in the air and it was braying noisily.

She thought this was the funniest sight she had ever seen and she burst out laughing! At once she cried out: "Father!" He was overjoyed to hear her speak. He rushed outside and brought Jack into the house – without the donkey of course!

His daughter fell in love with the fellow who had made her laugh so Lazy Jack married her. His mother went to live with them and they were all very happy together.

THE PRINCESS AND THE PEA

There was once a handsome prince who wanted to marry a princess – a *real* princess.

He travelled far and wide to find one and met a great many people, and quite a number of princesses, too. The trouble was that there was always something or other which appeared to be not quite right about the princesses, and after many months he returned home and told his parents, "I cannot find a princess to marry."

One night, not long after his return, a terrible storm broke over the palace. Lightning flashed, thunder crashed and the rain poured down. Suddenly, there was a loud knocking at the great front door. The prince and his parents looked at each other in surprise, "Who would be out in such a storm?" they asked. The old king went himself to see who was there.

A girl stood shivering on the doorstep. Water streamed off her hair and down her face and her dress was soaked through. "Come in," cried the king. "Come in and tell us who you are."

"I am a p-p-p-princess," she replied through her chattering teeth. "I was looking for the king's palace, and I was caught in a storm."

"Come and sit by the fire, dear child," said the king kindly. "You are wet through."

The shivering girl joined the queen and the prince at the big warm fire. The king told them that the girl had said she was a princess.

"But she doesn't look in the least like a princess!"

cried the queen. The prince thought she was very pretty, but wondered himself if she was a true princess.

"You must stay here tonight," the queen said to the girl, but secretly she thought: "I believe I can find out if she really is a princess or not."

While the girl was having a hot bath the queen went to prepare her bedroom. She sent two maids scurrying to collect mattresses and quilts from all over the palace. First she placed a dried pea underneath the bottom mattress and then more and more mattresses were piled onto the bed. In all, twenty mattresses were placed on top of the pea. Then the queen told the maids to place twenty feather quilts on top of the mattresses. "Now we shall see how well she sleeps!" said the queen.

When the girl went to the bedroom she found her bed so high that she had to climb a ladder to get into it.

The next morning both the king and queen asked if she had slept well.

"I am sorry to say, I had a very bad night," she told them. "There was a little hard lump in my bed and I tossed and turned all night. Now I am black and blue with bruises."

The queen was delighted. Only a real princess could have felt a pea through twenty mattresses and twenty quilts. She hurried off to tell the prince.

The prince was overjoyed at the news and asked the pretty princess to marry him at once. She was delighted to accept. They had a wonderful wedding and they lived happily together for many years.

As for the pea, it was put on display in a glass case in the town museum. When people saw it, they would say, "That really is some story, the story of the princess and the pea."

TWO OF EVERYTHING

Mr and Mrs Hak-Tak were rather old and rather poor. They had a small house in a village among the mountains and a tiny patch of green land on the mountainside. Here they grew the vegetables which were all they had to live on, and when it was a good season and they did not need to eat up everything as soon as it was grown, Mr Hak-Tak took what they could spare in a basket to the next village which was a little larger than theirs and sold it for as much as he could get and bought some oil for their lamp, and fresh seeds, and every now and then, but not often, a piece of cotton stuff to make new coats and trousers for himself and his wife. You can imagine they did not often get the chance to eat meat.

Now, one day it happened that when Mr Hak-Tak was digging in his precious patch, he unearthed a big brass pot. He thought it strange that it should have been there for so long without his having come across it before, and he was disappointed to find that it was empty; still, he thought they would find some use for it, so when he was ready to go back to the house in the evening he decided to take it with him. It was very big and heavy, and in his struggles to get his arms round it and raise it to a good position for carrying, his purse, which he always took with him in his belt, fell to the ground and to be quite sure he had it safe, he put it inside the pot and so staggered home with his load.

As soon as he got into the house Mrs Hak-Tak hurried from the inner room to meet him.

"My dear husband," she said, "whatever have you got there?"

"For a cooking pot it is too big; for a bath a little too small," said Mr Hak-Tak. "I found it buried in our vegetable patch and so far it has been useful in carrying my purse home for me."

"Alas," said Mrs Hak-Tak, "something smaller would have done as well to hold any money we have or are likely to have," and she stooped over the pot and looked into its dark inside.

As she stooped, her hairpin – for poor Mrs Hak-Tak had only one hairpin for all her hair and it was made of carved bone – fell into the pot. She put in her hand to get it out again, and then she gave a loud cry which brought her husband running to her side.

"What is it?" he asked. "Is there a viper in the pot?"

"Oh, my dear husband," she cried. "What can be the meaning of this? I put my hand into the pot to fetch out my hairpin and your purse, and look, I have brought out two hairpins and two purses, both exactly alike."

"Open the purse. Open both purses," said Mr Hak-Tak. "One of them will certainly be empty."

But not a bit of it. The new purse contained exactly the same number of coins as the old one – for that matter, no one could have said which was the new and which the old – and it meant, of course, that the Hak-Taks had exactly twice as much money in the evening as they had had in the morning.

"And two hairpins instead of one!" cried Mrs Hak-Tak, forgetting in her excitement to do up her hair which was streaming over her shoulders. "There is something quite unusual about this pot."

"Let us put in the sack of lentils and see what

happens," said Mr Hak-Tak, also becoming excited.

They heaved in the bag of lentils and when they pulled it out again – it was so big it almost filled the pot – they saw another bag of exactly the same size waiting to be pulled out in its turn. So now they had two bags of lentils instead of one.

"Put in the blanket," said Mr Hak-Tak. "We need another blanket for the cold weather." And, sure enough, when the blanket came out, there lay another behind it.

"Put my wadded coat in," said Mr Hak-Tak, "and then when the cold weather comes there will be one for you as well as for me. Let us put in everything we have in turn. What a pity we have no meat or tobacco, for it seems that the pot cannot make anything without a pattern."

Then Mrs Hak-Tak, who was a woman of great intelligence, said, "My dear husband, let us put the purse

in again and again and again. If we take two purses out each time we put one in, we shall have enough money by tomorrow evening to buy everything we lack."

"I am afraid we may lose it this time," said Mr Hak-Tak, but in the end he agreed, and they dropped in the purse and pulled out two, then they added the new money to the old and dropped it in again and pulled out the larger amount twice over. After a while the floor was covered with old leather purses and they decided just to throw the money in by itself. It worked quite as well and saved trouble; every time, twice as much money came out as went in, and every time they added the new coins to the old and threw them all in together. It took them some hours to tire of this game, but at last Mrs Hak-Tak said, "My dear husband, there is no need for us to work so hard. We shall see to it that the pot does not run away, and we can always make more money as we want it. Let us tie up what we have."

It made a huge bundle in the extra blanket and the Hak-Taks lay and looked at it for a long time before they slept, and talked of all the things they would buy and the improvements they would make in the cottage.

The next morning they rose early and Mr Hak-Tak filled a wallet with money from the bundle and set off for the big village to buy more things in one morning than he had bought in a whole fifty years.

Mrs Hak-Tak saw him off and then she tidied up the cottage and put the rice on to boil and had another look at the bundle of money, and made herself a whole set of new hairpins from the pot, and about twenty candles instead of the one which was all they had possessed up to now. After that she slept for a while, having been up so late the night before, but just before the time when her husband should be back, she awoke and went over to the pot. She dropped in a cabbage leaf to make sure it was till working properly, and when she took two leaves out she sat down on the floor and put her arms round it.

"I do not know how you came to us, my dear pot," she said, "but you are the best friend we ever had."

Then she knelt up to look inside it, and at that moment her husband came to the door, and, turning quickly to see all the wonderful things he had bought, she overbalanced and fell into the pot.

Mr Hak-Tak put down his bundles and ran across and caught her by the ankles and pulled her out, but, oh, mercy, no sooner had he set her carefully on the floor than he saw the kicking legs of another Mrs Hak-Tak in the pot! What was he to do? Well, he could not leave her there, so he caught her ankles and pulled, and another Mrs Hak-Tak so exactly like the first that no one would have told one from the other, stood beside them.

"Here's an extraordinary thing," said Mr Hak-Tak, looking helplessly from one to the other.

"I will not have a second Mrs Hak-Tak in the house!" screamed the old Mrs Hak-Tak.

All was confusion. The old Mrs Hak-Tak shouted and wrung her hands and wept, Mr Hak-Tak was scarcely calmer, and the new Mrs Hak-Tak sat down on the floor as if she knew no more than they did what was to happen next.

"One wife is all *I* want," said Mr Hak-Tak, "but how could I have left her in the pot?"

"Put her back in it again!" cried Mrs Hak-Tak.

"What? And draw out two more?" said her husband. "If two wives are too many for me, what should I do with three? No! No!" He stepped back quickly as if he was

stepping away from the three wives and, missing his footing, lo and behold, he fell into the pot!

Both Mrs Hak-Taks ran and each caught an ankle and pulled him out and set him on the floor, and there, oh, mercy, was another pair of kicking legs in the pot! Again each caught hold of an ankle and pulled, and soon another Mr Hak-Tak, so exactly like the first that no one could have told one from the other, stood beside them.

Now the old Mr Hak-Tak liked the idea of his double no more than Mrs Hak-Tak had liked the idea of hers. He stormed and raged and scolded his wife for pulling him out of the pot, while the new Mr Hak-Tak sat down on the floor beside the new Mrs Hak-Tak and looked as if, like her, he did not know what was going to happen next.

Then the old Mrs Hak-Tak had a very good idea.

"Listen, my dear husband," she said, "now, do stop scolding and listen, for it is really a good thing that there is a new one of you as well as a new one of me. It means that you and I can go on in our usual way, and these new people, who are ourselves and yet not ourselves, can set up house together next door to us."

And that is what they did. The old Hak-Taks built themselves a fine new house with money from the pot, and they built one just like it next door for the new couple, and they lived together in the greatest friendliness, because, as Mrs Hak-Tak said, "The new Mrs Hak-Tak is really more than a sister to me, and the new Mr Hak-Tak is really more than a brother to you."

The neighbours were very much surprised, both at the sudden wealth of the Hak-Taks and at the new couple who resembled them so strongly that they must, they thought, be very close relations of whom they had never heard before. They said: "It looks as though the Hak-Taks, when they so unexpectedly became rich, decided to have two of everything, even of themselves, in order to enjoy their money more."

BABOUSHKA

Once upon a time an old woman called Baboushka
lived in a little house deep in the forest. She lived all
alone but she was always busy cooking, cleaning, sewing,
chopping logs and she sang to herself all day long.

One winter's day there was a loud knock on her door.

"Who is there?" called Baboushka.

"We are weary travellers," a voice answered. "We
have lost our way and it is growing dark now. Can we rest
here for a while and get warm? Then if you'll tell us the
path to take, we'll be on our way."

At once Baboushka rushed to open the door. "Come
in," she said with a big smile, "and welcome to my
house."

One after the other, the travellers came in. There was
a young man first of all who bowed and smiled at her.
Then he turned and put his arm out to help an old man
who looked chilled and tired. The third man was neither
young nor old. He was tall with a fierce look on his face
and heavy gold rings in his ears. They shook the snow
from their rich embroidered clothes and stamped their
fine leather boots before they sat by the fire.

Baboushka bustled about and handed steaming hot
mugs of tea to them then she cut thick slices of her
home-made bread.

"Where are you going in this wintry weather?" she
asked.

They did not answer for a minute then the young man
said: "We don't know. It is not easy to explain. We are

looking for a baby prince but we do not know where he is. He sent a star to help us on our way but there is so much snow in the sky that we can't see it any more.''

"Well," said Baboushka, "I don't know any princes but I'll show you the road then you needn't worry about following a star!"

"Thank you," said the young man, "but only the star can lead us to the Christ-Child."

"A child? A star?" exclaimed Baboushka. "What do you mean?"

"The star means that a holy child will be born somewhere," the old man said. "Look, here are the presents we are taking for him."

"I wish I could see this child," Baboushka murmured.

"Come with us," all three cried. "Help us to look for him." Baboushka shook her head sadly. "I'm too old to travel," she said. Soon the men said they had to go. They thanked her for her kindness and she showed them the path to follow through the trees.

The house seemed quiet and empty. She rocked slowly in her rocking-chair. "I'd like to see this baby prince," she kept whispering. Suddenly she jumped to her feet.

"And I will go," she cried, "I'll join the search. I'll go tomorrow. So I will!"

She packed some warm clothes then she chose her greatest treasures to take to the holy child: a wooden horse, a cloth ball, an old doll, some painted fir cones and two pretty feathers.

Early next morning she wrapped up warmly and locked up. She tried to find the travellers' path but snow had covered their footsteps.

At last she met a shepherd.

"Have you seen a bright star?" she asked him eagerly.

"Thousands, old woman," he laughed. "Just look up. And they all shine brightly!"

A herdsman plodded past with his herd of cows.

"Have any baby princes been born here today?" Baboushka begged.

"Plenty of babies," he told her, "but not one of them a prince!"

She trudged on wearily. "Have you seen a Holy child?" she asked everyone she met. No one could help her.

Baboushka goes on searching to this very day; she travels looking for the Christ-Child. And whenever she meets a sick or unhappy child she manages to find a toy in her sack to make them smile happily again.

MUSICIANS OF BREMEN

One day an old donkey overheard his master saying that he was too old for work. The time had come for him to be killed off for they could not keep an animal who was no longer useful.

"Killed indeed!" snorted the donkey. "I may be too old to carry heavy loads but I am not too old to make a fine noise when I bray. I shall go to the neighbouring town of Bremen and earn my keep there as a musician."

He unlatched the stable door with his teeth, a trick he had learned long ago, and when no one was looking he slipped out and trotted down the road towards Bremen.

He had not gone far when he saw an old dog lying by the side of the road looking rather sorry for himself.

"Why so sad, Dog?" he asked.

"You would feel just as sad if you had overheard your master say he was going to knock you on the head because you were too old."

"Come with me, friend," said the donkey. "I am also too old for my master, so I am off to Bremen to earn my living as a musician. You can use your voice, can't you? Together we will sing a fine duet."

The dog agreed to travel to Bremen with the donkey, and they trotted down the road together. Before long, they saw a cat hunched up and miserable sitting on a gate.

"It's a fine day, Cat," they said, "too fine for you to look so sad."

"It's a bad sad day for me," said the cat. "My owners

say I no longer catch as many rats and mice as I did when I was young, so they are replacing me with a kitten. What is more, they said they could not afford to feed us both, so I am going to be put in a sack with a stone and drowned in the river."

"Don't wait for that to happen," said the donkey and the dog. "We are also too old for our masters, but we have not waited to be finished off. We are on our way to Bremen to earn our living as musicians. You still have your voice. Come with us."

The cat uttered a fine "Miaow!" in agreement.

So the three animals journeyed on to Bremen together. At the next farm they met a cock strutting up and down. All his feathers were ruffled out in indignation.

"What's the trouble, Cock?" they asked. "You look upset."

"How would you feel," replied the cock, "if you overheard your mistress planning to wring your neck so she could eat you for dinner on Sunday when they have visitors coming?"

"Come with us to Bremen," said the donkey, the dog and the cat. "We are going to earn our living there as musicians. We're sure you have a fine singing voice."

"Indeed I do," said the cock, and to show them he uttered a loud "Cock-a-doodle-doo!"

It was too far for them to reach Bremen that day, so when evening came they found a sheltered place in a wood to rest for the night. The dog and the donkey settled themselves comfortably at the bottom of a tree, the cat climbed into the branches, and the cock roosted high up at the top. They were all tired, but none of them slept for they were all so hungry.

When it was quite dark the animals saw a light

shining from a nearby house they had not noticed before. It made them think of food, and towards midnight the cat said, "Friends, let's go and investigate. Where there is a house, there may be something to eat."

Together they crept up to one of the windows where a light was shining. The donkey being the tallest looked through first.

"Well, friend, what do you see?" asked the cock.

"I see a table laden with food and drink, and a group of mean-looking men counting piles of money," said the donkey.

The cat, the dog and cockerel now jumped up onto the donkey's back and peered through the window too. They did not realize it but they had discovered a robber's hideout hidden deep in the woods.

"Let us try out our music," said one of the animals. "If we sing a fine song for them they may give us some of their supper."

Together they all sang. The donkey brayed, the dog barked, the cat yowled and the cock crowed. The noise was tremendous.

The effect was not at all what they expected, for the robbers, hearing this noise, thought they were about to be arrested. They ran helter-skelter as fast as they could into the woods, leaving the doors wide open.

"That was nice of them," said the four animals, when the robbers did not reappear. "They have gone away and left us their home to enjoy."

The donkey found some good hay in the barn and the cock some grain, while the cat and the dog ate all they wanted from the robbers' table. Then they all slept soundly. In time the candles burnt down and went out and the house lay in darkness.

Some hours later, the robbers returned. They had been arguing among themselves, for some thought they had given in too easily, by running away without a fight, while the others thought it was foolish to go back to the house, for they would surely be caught and put in prison. Now they drew nearer, and seeing no sign of life decided it would be safe for one of them to return and at least take some of the gold they had left behind.

Quietly the robber crept up to the house, and tried to light a candle. As he did so the cat awoke, and the robber saw his green eyes glowing in the dark. Mistaking them for the embers of the fire, he held out a splinter of wood to them.

The cat, thinking he was being attacked, flew at the robber, spitting and scratching for all he was worth. The robber, fearing some great wild beast was attacking him, dropped the wood and ran for his life. In the doorway he tripped over the dog who immediately bit the robber's ankle and howled in agony from the kick he had received. The robber ran headlong across the yard where the donkey lashed out his heels as he went past. The cock, hearing all the commotion and fearing his friends were being killed flew at the stranger, flapping his wings around his head, stretching out his claws and screeching all the time.

The robber fled back to his companions. "It is surely a monster and a devil rolled into one that has taken over our house," he said. "First I was scratched, then bitten, then kicked, and finally attacked from above by fierce talons and whirling feathers. The noise of screeching and howling was enough to wake the dead. We must never go back there again."

So it was that the robbers set off to another part of the country and left their hideout in the woods to the animals. Meanwhile the four musicians discussed in the morning the strange disturbances in the middle of the night. Since the intruder had disappeared they decided to stay where they were for a time.

"We will go to Bremen another day," they said.

But they never did go to Bremen. Instead they lived happily in the house for many years and never tried singing together again.

HENNY PENNY

One day Henny Penny was scratching in the farmyard looking for something good to eat when, suddenly, something hit her on the head.

"My goodness me!" she said. "The sky must be falling down. I must go and tell the king."

She had not gone far when she met her friend Cocky Locky.

"Where are you going in such a hurry?" he called out.

"I am going to tell the king that the sky is falling down," said Henny Penny.

"I will come with you," said Cocky Locky.

So Henny Penny and Cocky Locky hurried along together towards the king's palace. On the way they saw Ducky Lucky swimming on the pond. "Where are you going?" he called out.

"We are going to tell the king the sky is falling down," replied Henny Penny. "We must go quickly, as there is no time to lose."

"I will come with you," said Ducky Lucky, shaking the water off his feathers.

So Henny Penny, Cocky Locky and Ducky Lucky hurried on together towards the king's palace. On the way they met Goosey Loosey, who called out, "Where are you all going in such a hurry?"

"We are on our way to tell the king the sky is falling down," said Henny Penny.

"I will come with you," said Goosey Loosey.

So Henny Penny, Cocky Locky, Ducky Lucky and

Goosey Loosey hurried on together towards the king's palace.

Round the next corner they met Turkey Lurkey. "Where are you all going on this fine day?" she called out to them.

"It won't be a fine day for long," replied Henny Penny. "The sky is falling down, and we are hurrying to tell the king."

"I will come with you," said Turkey Lurkey.

So Henny Penny, Cocky Locky, Ducky Lucky, Goosey Loosey and Turkey Lurkey all went on towards the king's palace.

Now on their way they met Foxy Loxy who asked, "Where are you going in such a hurry?"

"We are going to the king's palace to tell him the sky is falling down," replied Henny Penny.

"That is a very important message," said Foxy Loxy.

"I will come with you. In fact if you follow me I can show you a short cut to the king's palace, so you will get there sooner."

So Henny Penny, Cocky Locky, Ducky Lucky, Goosey Loosey and Turkey Lurkey all followed Foxy Loxy. He led them to the wood, and up to a dark hole, which was the door to his home. Inside his wife and five hungry children were waiting for him to bring home some dinner.

That, I am sorry to say, was the end of Cocky Locky, Ducky Lucky, Goosey Loosey and Turkey Lurkey, for one by one they all followed Foxy Loxy into his home, and they were all eaten up by the hungry fox family.

Henny Penny was the last to enter the Fox's hole and she heard Cocky Locky crowing in alarm in front of her. Squawking with fright and scattering feathers, she turned and ran as fast as she could for the safety of her own farmyard. There she stayed and she never did tell the king that the sky was falling down.

HANS IN LUCK

A young man called Hans worked very hard for seven years so he went to his master and said: "I've learnt to do my work and I'd like to go home to see my mother. Please give me my wages."

"You have worked well, Hans," his master said. "Your work is good so your pay shall be good." And he gave Hans a lump of gold as big as his head! Hans wrapped it up in his spotted handkerchief and put it on his head. His master gave him some food and he trudged off.

After he had walked a few miles his feet felt sore and he went slower and slower. Before long he saw a man riding on a fine horse.

"Oh dear," sighed Hans, "what a good thing it is to ride on horseback. That man looks as comfortable as if he were sitting at home by the fire! He doesn't trip over stones; he doesn't wear out his boots and his horse knows the right road too."

The horseman heard Hans grumbling and he said:

"Well, my friend, if you feel like that, why are you walking?"

"It's like this," said Hans, "I've got to carry this big lump of gold and it is so heavy that I can't hold up my head and it's making my shoulders very sore."

"I have a good idea," said the rider. "Why don't you give me your gold and you shall have my horse. That will save you a lot of trouble."

"With all my heart," said Hans. The horseman

156

laughed and he jumped down. He took the lump of gold, helped Hans into the saddle and put the whip and reins into his hands.

"When you want to go fast," he explained, "just click your tongue and shout 'Gee-up!'"

Hans was delighted. He cracked the whip and the horse trotted away. Hans wanted to go faster so he shouted "Gee-up!" Away went the horse. Off fell Hans, straight into a ditch!

The horse went off by itself and a young man walking by with a cow, stopped it. Hans got to his feet. "It's no joke trying to ride a horse like that. It threw me off as if it wanted to break my neck! I won't ride it again in a hurry. Your cow looks much quieter. I could walk behind her and she'd give me milk, butter and cheese every day without any trouble. I wish I had a fine cow."

"Well," said the young man, "if you like her so much I'll change my cow for your horse."

"Done," exclaimed Hans. The other jumped on the horse and galloped away as fast as he could!

Hans drove the cow along, very pleased with his bargain.

"Why," he told himself, "I'll never be hungry with butter and cheese with my bread and I can milk the cow when I am thirsty." He ate his food and walked on but before long he was hot and dusty.

"I'll milk the cow and get a drink!" he said. He tied her to a tree and put his leather bag underneath to catch the milk. But not a single drop appeared. Then the cow gave him a hard kick and he fell over backwards!

A man with a pig came past at that moment. "What happened?" he asked as he helped Hans to get up. "I only wanted some milk," replied Hans.

"Milk!" the man said. "That cow is too old to give you any milk."

"Oh dear, I gave away a good horse for this miserable cow. She is no use to me for I don't like beef. Now with a pig, I'd get bacon and sausages!

"I like to help when I can," said the man, "so I'll give you my pig for that cow if you like."

"You are a good friend," said Hans. And he led the pig away with a string round its neck.

Hans whistled as he strolled along and soon he met a man carrying a large white goose. They stopped to chat and Hans told him about the lucky exchanges he had made.

"Feel my fine goose," the man said. "It will make a good dinner for it is plump and juicy."

"You're right," said Hans, "but my pig is just as fine."

The other man shook his head. "You seem to be an honest fellow so I'm sorry to tell you that your pig looks like the one stolen from that farm over there. You'll be in terrible trouble if the farmer catches you."

"Dear me," Hans was frightened. "What shall I do?"

"I'd like to help you," answered the man.

"Take my pig then," said Hans, "and give me your goose." The man agreed and he led the pig away as quickly as he could. Hans was pleased. "I can roast this goose and put the soft white feathers into a pillow. I'll sleep well on such a fine pillow!"

He was nearly home when he met a scissors grinder who was turning his wheel and singing a song.

"You seem happy, Mister Grinder," Hans said.

"Yes," was the reply. "I've always got plenty of work so there's always gold in my pocket. That's a fine goose you have. Where did you buy it?"

"I didn't buy it; I changed my pig for it."

"Where did you get the pig?"

"I gave my cow for it."

"And the cow?"

"My horse went for the cow."

"And the horse?"

"I gave a lump of gold as big as my head for it."

"And the gold?"

"That was my pay for seven years' hard work."

"Well," said the grinder, "you have done well so far. Wouldn't it be better if you always had money in your pocket? Your fortune would be made."

"That's true," said Hans, "but how can I do that?"

"Why not be a scissors-grinder? I have a spare stone here. I don't want any money but I'd like your goose. Will you change with me?"

"What a question!" replied Hans. "With my pockets full of money, I'd be happy! What more do I want? Here, take my goose." He did not see the grinder pick up an

ordinary stone from the path! "This is an excellent stone," he told Hans. "You can even make bent nails straight if you hammer them with it."

Hans took the stone and went on cheerfully. "I am a lucky fellow," he thought.

He began to feel weary for the stone was twice as heavy as a lump of gold. When he came to a sparkling river he threw himself down on the bank for a rest. Carefully, he put down the stone then he stooped over to have a drink. The cool water tasted so good that Hans forgot about the stone and by mistake, he pushed against it and down it rolled *splash*, *splash*, into the water. Hans watched as it sank deeper and deeper and when it disappeared he jumped to his feet and danced around with joy!

"I have nothing to worry about now, for that big heavy stone has gone!"

He forgot that he was tired and he ran and ran until he was safe and sound at his mother's house.

PRINCESS UNDER THE EARTH

There was once a very rich king who had the most beautiful daughter in the world. He built a wonderful palace for her but he hid it under the earth. On his daughter's seventeenth birthday he shut her up inside this palace with her ladies-in-waiting. Then he sent his servants to every corner of the world with this message:

"The first young man to find the hidden princess will take her as his wife. He may only try once. If he cannot find her, he will die."

Princes and nobles searched for the princess but not one of them managed to find the hiding-place so they were beheaded. Soon nobody wanted to look for the princess until one day a clever young man decided to try his luck. First he went to a shepherd.

"Will you hide me in a gold fleece and carry me to the king?" he asked.

"Yes, certainly," the shepherd replied and he covered the young man with a golden lamb's fleece. He sewed it neatly so that it looked like a golden lamb. Then he took it to the king who said:

"What a beautiful lamb! I'd like to buy it."

"I'm sorry, your majesty," said the shepherd, "I'm afraid I cannot sell it. But if you promise to give it back, I'll lend it to you for three days."

The king promised, then he took the lamb to show his daughter. He walked through many rooms and passages in her palace until he reached a heavily bolted door. He knocked *trrum-trrum-trree* and called:

161

"Unbolt yourself and open wide, O Door of Iron!"

It flung itself open. He walked through more rooms until at last he came to another strong iron door, and he cried again:

"Unbolt yourself and open wide, O Door of Iron!"

This time he went into a room with walls made of silver where the most beautiful princess in the world was sitting. He showed her the golden lamb which she stroked gently before she carried it to her bedroom. When the princess was alone, the young man unstitched the lamb-skin and stood in front of her. She fell in love with him at once and clapped her hands together in delight.

"How clever you are! But be careful. My father will have another hard test for you. He'll change me and my ladies into ducks. Then he'll ask you to guess which duck is the princess! Listen carefully and I'll tell you how to

choose the right one. I'll be the duck which turns its head to smooth its feathers. Don't forget!"

After three days the shepherd asked the king for his lamb. The shepherd carried away the lamb but as soon as the king could not see them, the young man stepped out of the lamb-skin. He went straight back to the king.

"I want to look for your daughter," he told him.

The king liked the look of this bright young man.

"Think carefully. You will die if you don't find her."

"I'm willing to give my life for the chance," was the reply.

So the young man set off and led the king through the many doors and passages of the underground palace until they came to the first door. Then he said:

"Your Majesty, you must say these special words now."

"What words do you mean?" the king asked.

"You must say 'Unbolt yourself and open wide, O Door of Iron.'"

It opened at once. The second door opened in the same way and they went into the lovely silver room where his daughter and her ladies were sitting.

"Well," said the king, "you've found my daughter but you can't marry her yet!"

In a flash, the princess and her ladies were turned into pretty fluffy ducks.

"There you are," laughed the king, "which is the princess?"

"There she is," the young man said, pointing to the duck which was smoothing its feathers with its beak.

The clever young man and the princess were married next day and lived happily together – in a proper palace this time!

A Very Big Cat

Many years ago a hunter from the Northlands caught a great white bear. It was such a fine bear that he decided to present it to the king of his country. So on Christmas Eve the man and the bear set out. It was winter and the snow was falling thick and fast. They grew tired after a while and stopped at a little cottage to ask for shelter. The door was opened by a tall thin man with a very worried face.

"Please may we come in? We are both very tired with trudging through the snow," said the hunter.

"Oh no, no," replied the man whose name was Halvor.

"We are going to see the king, this fine bear and I. We only want to warm ourselves at your fire for the night."

"Impossible! You can't stay here. I'm not an unkind man. I'd like to help you, but it's Christmas Eve, a time of great trouble for me." He opened the door wider. "Look at my wife and my three children hurrying to get things ready for Christmas. See how sad and worried they look," Halvor went on. "They never enjoy Christmas because year after year the trolls come. Many, many trolls. They chase us out, throw our food about, then break all the dishes. They tear down the decorations, they scream, they shout. Oh no, Christmas is not a happy time for us."

"Trolls!" exclaimed the hunter. "Trolls don't frighten us. Please let us into your warm house."

At last Halvor let them both in and they slept in a warm corner near the stove. Halvor's wife had prepared a delicious dinner and on Christmas Day she put everything on the table, which the children decorated with holly and candles. All of a sudden, quicker than a flash, the trolls appeared. They came down the chimney, in at the windows, under the door and even up through the floorboards. Some were tall and some were small. Some had long noses and no tails; some had long tails and long ears. All of them were very, very ugly. Halvor and his family grabbed their warmest clothes and ran and locked themselves in the woodshed.

Then those trolls attacked. They bellowed. They screamed. They threw the turkey and vegetables about and smashed the dishes. They squashed jellies into the floor and blew bubbles in the milk. They jumped on the table and paddled in the custard. Some smaller trolls emptied jars of jam and rubbed it over the windows. The noise was terrible but the man and his bear watched quietly by the stove. At last, when there was nothing left to damage, the naughtiest troll of all saw the big bear lying peacefully in the corner. He grabbed a sausage, pushed it on a fork and waved it under the bear's nose.

"Pussy, pussy, have a sausage," he shouted in a silly voice. The bear sniffed. It was a good smell. At once the troll pulled the sausage away, out of the bear's reach.

"Pussy, pussy, here you are." Again the troll waved the sausage in front of the bear and again he snatched it away. Slowly the bear lumbered to his feet. He opened his mouth wider and wider. He let out a great roar, then another even louder one. He chased those trolls up the chimney, out of the windows and under the floorboards, until there was not one left.

"You are a fine bear," the hunter said proudly. "Here, have a sausage or two." So the bear ate the sausages; then he licked some jam from the windows because bears love sweet things.

"You can come out of the woodshed now," the hunter shouted. "My bear has chased away all the trolls."

Halvor, his wife and three children crept back to the cottage. They could hardly believe the trolls had gone, but when they saw it was true they set about cleaning up the mess with a will. There was enough food for a good supper before they all went to bed, and the next day the hunter and the bear went on their way to the king.

A year later, on Christmas Eve, Halvor was chopping wood in the forest when he heard someone calling him.

"Is that big white cat still living with you?" It was a troll's voice.

"She certainly is," shouted Halvor. "And she has seven kittens now, each one bigger and fiercer than the last. Do you want to visit her?"

"No! We'll never come to your house again," the trolls screamed. And they never did. Ever afterwards Halvor, his wife and their three children enjoyed their Christmas Day in peace and contentment.

LITTLE LISA

Once upon a time a little girl called Lisa lived in a little red house in a country called Sweden. Little Lisa's mother made her a beautiful green dress with a red and white striped apron to wear over it. She had a red cloak and a bright blue scarf and her father bought her a pair of red shoes and a shiny green umbrella.

She looked very pretty in her new clothes. "I think I'm the prettiest girl in Sweden," Lisa thought.

One day her mother said: "I've baked a cake for your grandmother. Why don't you put on your pretty new clothes and take it to her? It isn't far if you follow the path through the forest. You'll soon be there."

Lisa was delighted. She loved visiting her grandmother as she told Lisa lots of wonderful fairy stories.

Quickly she changed her clothes and picked up her basket. "I'll stay on the road," she promised, "and I'm taking my new umbrella to show grandmother."

She kissed her mother goodbye and set off. It was shady and pleasant in the forest and Lisa spotted some wild strawberries growing by the roadside.

"They look good," she said as she knelt down to pick them.

They were sweet and juicy and as she wandered further among the trees, the strawberries got redder and sweeter. Soon she was deep inside the forest.

"I promised not to leave the road," she sobbed. "Now I'm lost and frightened. What shall I do?"

Then she heard a deep growl and she saw a big brown bear ambling towards her.

"Grr, grr! I'm going to eat you all up," growled the bear.

"Please don't do that," begged Little Lisa. "You can have my red-striped apron and my blue scarf if you promise to let me go."

The bear nodded. "I won't eat you if you hand over your apron and scarf."

So she gave them to the bear and away he went.

"I'm the prettiest bear in the forest," he sang in his growly voice.

Little Lisa did not know which way to go and she burst into tears. A terrible howl made her jump and she saw a fearsome wolf beside her.

"I'm going to eat you all up," he said, smacking his lips.

"Please don't do that," begged Little Lisa again, "You can have my new green dress if you promise to let me go."

"Your dress is too small for a big wolf like me."

"It will make a nice head-dress," said Little Lisa and she wrapped it round his head.

"I'm the most beautiful wolf in the forest," he howled proudly as he ran away.

"I'd better keep walking," Little Lisa said. "Perhaps I can find my way home." Another strange noise startled her and this time a red fox with a long tail stood in her path.

"You will make a nice supper!" he said. "I'm going to eat you all up."

"Please don't do that," Little Lisa begged for the third time. "You can have my shiny green umbrella if you will promise to let me go."

"I've never had an umbrella," said the fox, "so I'll take yours and hunt for another supper! I'm the finest fox in the forest." And away he lolloped.

Poor Little Lisa had lost all her new clothes except her cloak. She'd left her basket on the roadside too. She sat down and cried but it grew darker and darker. "I'd better start walking," she thought. I expect my poor grandmother is waiting for her cake but she won't get it tonight!"

She came to a big stone so she sat down to have a rest. "I wonder what mother is doing? I wish I could see her," said Little Lisa and she sobbed once again. Suddenly she felt a soft little paw touching her foot.

"What is the matter, little girl? Why are you crying?" A little fluffy rabbit was sitting next to her.

169

"Please answer me," he said, twitching his long whiskers. "I'm in rather a hurry, you see. Oh, I like your pretty shoes. I'm sure they'd make me run faster. Will you give them to me please?"

"Don't you want to eat me?" asked Little Lisa.

"Of course not!" said the rabbit. "I like running, not eating."

"Here you are, dear rabbit," Little Lisa said, "I won't need red shoes now that I've lost my beautiful clothes. I'll put them on for you if you like."

"They are so pretty," the rabbit was pleased. "What a kind little girl you are. Would you like to get on my back then we can see how fast I can run now."

So Little Lisa climbed up and away they went. They flew over the ground and she held onto the rabbit's ears as she didn't want to fall off! They were going lippity, loppity along when they heard a horrible noise.

"Oh dear," cried Little Lisa, "that sounds like the bear, the wolf and the fox coming to eat me. Please hurry, dear rabbit."

"Don't worry, Little Lisa," he said, "I am the fastest runner in the forest. But let us first find out what that noise is all about."

The two of them hid behind a tree. Little Lisa peeped out and to her surprise she saw the bear, the wolf and the fox standing there.

"I tell you, I'm the most beautiful animal in the forest," shouted the bear.

"No, no, you are not," said the fox, "look at my beautiful tail."

"What about my wonderful head and ears," said the wolf.

They argued and they shouted then the bear tore off

Little Lisa's red and white striped apron and blue scarf.

"I'm ready to fight you both," he growled. Off came Lisa's dress from the wolf's head. The fox threw down his green umbrella then they started fighting furiously.

The fox ran round a big tree so the bear grabbed his long bushy tail. The fox tugged at the wolf's tail and the wolf caught hold of the bear's short stubby tail. Round and round the tree the three animals ran, faster and faster.

Little Lisa crept out and picked up all her clothes.

"You don't deserve to have my pretty clothes," she whispered. The bear, the wolf and the fox did not notice her. Brr, brr, grr, grr, growl, growl they were shouting as they chased each other angrily. Little Lisa put on her clothes and ran to the rabbit.

"We'd better go before they see us," she said as she

climbed on his back. "Please take me home. My mother will give you hot pancakes and jam!"

"Mmm, I can smell them already!" said the rabbit as he scampered along.

Soon they arrived home. Lisa's mother was very surprised to see her daughter riding on a rabbit but she was unhappy when Little Lisa told her about the bear, the wolf and the fox!

"You shouldn't have left the road. You were lucky to escape," she said. "Still, you're safe and sound thanks to this kind little rabbit so we'll have a pancake party." She made heaps and heaps of pancakes and flipped them in the air and caught them in the pan!

Then Little Lisa, her father and mother and the little rabbit sat down and ate all those lovely pancakes, dripping with jam, honey and syrup. And Lisa promised to visit her grandmother the very next day and not stray from the path again.

THE ELEPHANT AND THE BAD BABY

Once upon a time there was an Elephant. And one day the Elephant went for a walk and he met a Bad Baby. And the Elephant said to the Bad Baby, "Would you like a ride?" And the Bad Baby said, "Yes."

So the Elephant stretched out his trunk, and picked up the Bad Baby and put him on his back, and they went rumpeta, rumpeta, rumpeta, all down the road.

Very soon they met an ice-cream man. And the Elephant said to the Bad Baby, "Would you like an ice-cream?" And the Bad Baby said, "Yes."

So the Elephant stretched out his trunk and took an ice-cream for himself and an ice-cream for the Bad Baby, and they went rumpeta, rumpeta, rumpeta, all down the road, with the ice-cream man running after.

Next they came to a pork butcher's shop. And the Elephant said to the Bad Baby, "Would like a pie?" And the Bad Baby said, "Yes."

So the Elephant stretched out his trunk and took a pie for himself and a pie for the Bad Baby, and they went rumpeta, rumpeta, rumpeta, all down the road, with the ice-cream man and the pork butcher both running after.

Next they came to a baker's shop. And the Elephant said to the Bad Baby, "Would you like a bun?" And the Bad Baby said, "Yes."

So the Elephant stretched out his trunk and took a bun for himself and a bun for the Bad Baby, and they went rumpeta, rumpeta, rumpeta, all down the road, with the ice-cream man, and the pork butcher, and the baker all running after.

Next they came to a snack bar. And the Elephant said to the Bad Baby, "Would you like some crisps?" And the Bad Baby said, "Yes."

So the Elephant stretched out his trunk and took some crisps for himself and some crisps for the Bad Baby, and they went rumpeta, rumpeta, rumpeta, all down the road, with the ice-cream man, and the pork butcher, and the baker, and the snack bar man all running after.

Next they came to a grocer's shop. And the Elephant said to the Bad Baby, "Would you like a chocolate biscuit?" And the Bad Baby said, "Yes."

So the Elephant stretched out his trunk and took a chocolate biscuit for himself and a chocolate biscuit for the Bad Baby, and they went rumpeta, rumpeta,

rumpeta, all down the road, with the ice-cream man, and the pork butcher, and the baker, and the snack bar man, and the grocer all running after.

Next they came to a sweet shop. And the Elephant said to the Bad Baby, "Would you like a lollipop?" And the Bad Baby said, "Yes."

So the Elephant stretched out his trunk and took a lollipop for himself and a lollipop for the Bad Baby and they went rumpeta, rumpeta, rumpeta, all down the road, with the ice-cream man, and the pork butcher, and the baker, and the snack bar man, and the grocer, and the lady from the sweet shop all running after.

Next they came to a fruit barrow. And the Elephant said to the Bad Baby, "Would you like an apple?" And the Bad Baby said, "Yes."

So the Elephant stretched out his trunk and took an apple for himself and an apple for the Bad Baby, and they went rumpeta, rumpeta, rumpeta, all down the road, with the ice-cream man, and the pork butcher, and the baker, and the snack bar man, and the grocer, and the lady from the sweet shop, and the barrow boy all running after.

Then the Elephant said to the Bad Baby, "But you haven't once said please!" And then he said, "You haven't ONCE said please!"

Then the Elephant sat down suddenly in the middle of the road and the Bad Baby fell off.

And the ice-cream man, and the pork butcher, and the baker, and the snack bar man, and the grocer, and the lady from the sweet shop, and the barrow boy all went BUMP into a heap.

And the Elephant said, "But he never once said please!"

And the ice-cream man, and the pork butcher, and the baker, and the snack bar man, and the grocer, and the lady from the sweet shop, and the barrow boy all picked themselves up and said, "Just fancy that! He never *once* said please!"

And the Bad Baby said: "PLEASE! I want to go home to my Mummy!"

So the Elephant stretched out his trunk, and picked up the Bad Baby and put him on his back, and they went rumpeta, rumpeta, rumpeta, all down the road, with the ice-cream man, and the pork butcher, and the baker, and the snack bar man, and the grocer, and the lady from the sweet shop, and the barrow boy all running after.

When the Bad Baby's Mummy saw them, she said, "Have you all come for tea?" And they all said, "Yes, *please!"* So they all went in and had tea, and the Bad Baby's Mummy made pancakes for everybody.

Then the Elephant went rumpeta, rumpeta, rumpeta, all down the road, with the ice-cream man, and the butcher, and the baker, and the snack bar man, and the grocer, and the lady from the sweet shop, and the barrow boy all running after.

But the Bad Baby went to bed.

THE WOOD FAIRY

Once upon a time a little girl called Betushka lived with her mother in a little cottage. They were poor but they were happy with their spinning and their two goats.

One day Betushka, as usual, packed some bread and a spindle in her bag. She drove their two goats to a grassy place in the birch wood and all the way there she sang and danced. The goats nibbled the grass and Betushka started to spin. All the time she sang happily.

At mid-day she ate her bread and the goats wandered up to take some from her hand. She jumped up and danced for a time and then she started spinning again.

A little later she got up to dance once more. Suddenly a lovely maiden stood before her. Her white silken dress floated like a cloud and a wreath of sweet-smelling flowers held back her long golden hair. She smiled at the frightened little girl.

"Do you like dancing?" she asked.

"Oh," she replied, "I'd like to dance all day!"

"Then we shall dance together. Come, I will teach you."

She held out her hand and they danced together. The maiden asked all the birds to sing their sweetest songs and their music filled the air. Betushka forgot about the goats and her spinning as she danced. Then the sunlight faded behind the trees. The birdsong stopped and the maiden disappeared instantly!

Betushka picked up her spindle. It was only half-filled

with thread. Sadly she put it into her bag and drove the goats home.

"I won't tell mother about the maiden," she said to herself, "I'll hide this spindle for it was wrong of me to waste time today. I'll work twice as hard tomorrow."

So early next day, Betushka, with her goats, went to the wood. She sang as she worked and at noon she shared her bread with the goats. "Why don't you dance, little goats?" she asked, "For today I must work hard."

"Little girl, come and dance," called a voice. It was the lovely maiden!

"I must finish my spinning," said Betushka, "for my mother needs the thread to weave cloth to sell. I cannot dance today."

"You can dance and someone will help you to spin," promised the maiden. The birds began singing their sweet songs so Betushka jumped to her feet and danced all afternoon. Then she noticed her half-empty spindle. She burst into tears.

At once, the maiden wound the flax around a silvery birch tree. She seized the spindle and began to spin. The spindle hummed as it twirled around and in a flash, the flax was spun and the spindle was full. The maiden sang:

> *"Wind it and grumble not,*
> *Wind it and grumble not."*

Then she vanished.

Betushka sang as she went home and gave a full spindle to her mother.

"I could only find a half-spindle this morning," her mother said, "so I could not weave very much. Whatever happened to you?"

"I'm truly sorry, mother," her daughter replied, "I danced instead of working all the time." She did not tell her about the maiden.

She went even earlier to the birch wood next day. She sang, spun and watched her goats and at mid-day the maiden appeared. Betushka forgot her promise to work hard and she danced with the maiden while the birds sang in the trees. The sun was setting before Betushka remembered her work. What was she to do! She began to cry and the maiden said kindly: "Take this. It is your bag but remember, do not open it until you get home." With that she vanished once more.

As she walked home behind the goats, Betushka was puzzled and a little frightened. Her bag felt very light so she peeped inside. The spindle was there. It was only half-full and the bag was full of dry birch leaves! She threw some away angrily then she stopped.

"I'd better take them home," she decided, "for the

goats can sleep on these leaves. But I wonder what mother will say to me?"

Oh dear, mother was waiting at the door, and did not look very pleased.

"What did you do to that spindle yesterday?" she demanded. "No matter how much cloth I made, the spindle stayed full of thread. 'An evil goblin did this.' I grumbled and as I said that, the thread vanished. What does this mean?"

Betushka was happy for she saw that her mother was not cross with her so she told her about the maiden, the music, the dancing and the filling of the spindles.

"You've seen a Wood Fairy!" her mother told her. "They dance at mid-day and midnight. Sometimes they are wicked but mostly they give lovely presents to people they like."

She smiled at her daughter. "I wish you'd told me about it. I could have filled the cottage with thread and

cloth if I hadn't grumbled!"

Then Betushka remembered her bag. First, she lifted out the spindle and flax.

"Oh," she gasped, "just look here, mother!"

All those dry old birch leaves had turned into gold. They clapped their hands and hugged each other.

"There is something more to tell," the girl said. "The Wood Fairy told me not to open my bag until I got home. I was so worried because I hadn't filled the spindle so I opened it and I threw out some of the leaves." She hung her head.

"What a good thing you didn't throw the whole bagfull out," her mother exclaimed.

The gold leaves gave them enough money to buy a farm with cows and a beautiful garden. Betushka and her mother were never poor again. When the birds sang in the wood, Betushka would sometimes dance but she never saw the Wood Fairy ever again.

THE LITTLE RED HEN

Once upon a time there was a little red hen. She lived with a pig, a duck and a cat.

They all lived in a pretty little house which the little red hen liked to keep clean and tidy. The little red hen worked hard at her jobs all day. The others never helped. Although they said they meant to, they were all far too lazy. The pig liked to grunt in the mud outside, the duck used to swim in the pond all day, and the cat enjoyed lying in the sun, purring.

One day the little red hen was working in the garden when she found a grain of corn.

"Who will plant this grain of corn?" she asked.

"Not I," grunted the pig from his muddy patch in the garden.

"Not I," quacked the duck from her pond.

"Not I," purred the cat from his place in the sun.

So the little red hen went to look for a nice bit of earth, scratched it with her feet and planted the grain of corn.

During the summer the grain of corn grew. First it grew into a tall green stalk, then it ripened in the sun until it had turned a lovely golden colour. The little red hen saw that the corn was ready for cutting.

"Who will help me cut the corn?" asked the little red hen.

"Not I," grunted the pig from his muddy patch in the garden.

"Not I," quacked the duck from her pond.

"Not I," purred the cat from his place in the sun.

"Very well then, I will cut it myself," said the little red hen. Carefully she cut the stalk and took out all the grains of corn from the husks.

"Who will take the corn to the mill, so that it can be ground into flour?" asked the little red hen.

"Not I," grunted the pig from his muddy patch in the garden.

"Not I," quacked the duck from her pond.

"Not I," purred the cat from his place in the sun.

So the little red hen took the corn to the mill herself, and asked the miller if he would be so kind as to grind it into flour.

In time the miller sent a little bag of flour down to the house where the little red hen lived with the pig and the duck and the cat.

"Who will help me to make the flour into bread?" asked the little red hen.

"Not I," grunted the pig from his muddy patch in the garden.

"Not I," quacked the duck from her pond.

"Not I," purred the cat from his place in the sun.

"Very well," said the little red hen. "I shall make the bread myself." She went into her neat little kitchen. She mixed the flour into dough. She kneaded the dough and put it into the oven to bake.

Soon there was a lovely smell of hot fresh bread. It filled all the corners of the house and wafted out into the garden. The pig came into the kitchen from his muddy patch in the garden, the duck came in from the pond and the cat left his place in the sun. When the little red hen opened the oven door the dough had risen up and had turned into the nicest, most delicious looking loaf of bread any of them had seen.

"Who is going to eat this bread?" asked the little red hen.

"I will," grunted the pig.

"I will," quacked the duck.

"I will," purred the cat.

"Oh no, you won't," said the little red hen. "I planted the seed, I cut the corn, I took it to the mill to be made into flour, and I made the bread, all by myself. I shall now eat the loaf all by myself."

The pig, the duck and the cat all stood and watched as the little red hen ate the loaf all by herself. It was delicious and she enjoyed it, right to the very last crumb.

THE HARE
AND THE TORTOISE

In the forest there was a clearing where many animals gathered each evening after going to the river to drink. The tortoise was usually the last to arrive, and the other animals would laugh at him as he plodded into the clearing.

"Come on, Slowcoach," they would call out as he came through the grass towards them. The tortoise would blink at them with his beady eyes and continue slowly on his way until he reached the spot where he wanted to settle down.

The liveliest of all the animals there was the hare. He ran so fast that he was always the first to arrive. "Just look at me," he was boasting one evening, "I can run faster than any of you. My speed and cleverness will always win."

The tortoise ambled into the clearing, last as usual. But to everyone's surprise he did not go to his usual place. Instead he went slowly across to the hare.

"Since you run so fast, could you beat me in a race?" he asked.

"*I* beat *you*, in a *race!*" exclaimed the hare, and he fell on the ground and held his sides he laughed so much. "Of course I would beat you. You name the distance, Tortoise, but don't make it too far for your short little legs," and he roared with laughter again.

Most of the other animals laughed too. It did seem a very comic idea. The fox who thought they would see some good sport said,

"Come on then, Tortoise, name the distance and the time and then we will all come to see fair play."

"Let us start tomorrow morning, at sunrise," suggested the tortoise. "We'll run from this clearing to the edge of the forest and return to this spot again along the bank of the river."

"Why, it will take you all day to go so far, Tortoise. Are you sure you want to go ahead with it?" asked the hare. He grinned all over his face at the thought of the easy victory he would have.

"I am sure," replied the tortoise. "The first one back to this clearing will be the winner."

"Agreed!" said the hare, as the tortoise settled down in some long grass to sleep for the night.

The next morning the clearing was full of animals who had come to see the start of the great race. Some ran along to the edge of the forest to make sure that both animals followed the proper route. Others chose good places to watch along the way. The hare and the tortoise stood side by side. As the sun rose, the fox called out,

"Ready, steady, go!"

The hare jumped up and was out of sight almost at once. The tortoise started off in the same direction. He plodded along picking up his feet slowly, then putting them down only a little in front of where they had been before.

"Come on, Tortoise," called his friends anxiously. But he did not lift up his foot to wave at them as the hare had done. He kept on moving slowly forwards.

In a few minutes the hare was a long way from the starting line so he slowed down. "It's going to take the tortoise all day," he thought, "so there is no need for me to hurry." He stopped to talk to friends and nibble juicy grass here and there along the path.

By the time he reached half way the sun was high in the sky and the day became very hot. The animals who were waiting there saw the hare turn back towards the clearing. They settled down for a long wait for the tortoise.

As he returned by the river, the hot sun and the grass he had eaten made the hare feel sleepy.

"There's no need to hurry," he told himself. "Here's a nice shady spot," and stretching himself comfortably, he lay down. With paws beneath his head, he murmured sleepily, "It won't matter if Tortoise passes me, I'm much faster than he is. I'll still get back first and win the race." He drifted off to sleep.

Meanwhile the tortoise went on slowly. He reached the edge of the forest quite soon after the hare, for he had not stopped to talk to friends or eat the tempting fresh grass along the path. Before long, smiling gently, he

passed the hare sleeping in the shade.

The animals in the clearing waited all day for the hare to return, but he did not arrive. The sun was setting before they saw the tortoise plodding towards them.

"Where is the hare?" they called out. The tortoise did not waste his breath in answering but came steadily towards them.

"Hurrah, Tortoise has won. Well done, Slowcoach!" the animals cheered. Only when he knew he had won the race did Tortoise speak,

"Hare? Oh, he's asleep back there by the river."

There was a sudden flurry and at great speed the hare burst into the clearing. He had woken and, seeing how long the shadows were, realized he had slept for much longer than he intended. He had raced back to the clearing but he was too late.

Tortoise smiled and said, "Slow and steady wins the race."

SNOW-WHITE AND ROSE-RED

A poor woman once lived with her two daughters in a pretty cottage at the edge of a forest. In the garden there were two rose-bushes, one with white flowers and the other with red ones so the woman's little daughters were called Snow-white and Rose-red like the roses.

Snow-white was fair-haired while Rose-red had black hair. The girls were very fond of each other. They went everywhere hand in hand and their mother loved them dearly.

One evening snow and ice covered the ground outside but inside the fire glowed and it was warm and cosy as the mother read stories to her children. Suddenly there was a loud knock at the door.

"Open the door, Rose-red," the mother said, "a traveller must have lost his way. He'll be half-frozen for it is bitterly cold tonight."

Rose-red opened the door. She screamed and jumped back. A big black shaggy bear put his head inside!

"Don't be afraid," he growled. "I won't hurt you. I only want to warm myself at your fire."

"Poor bear," the mother said, "come and lie down by the fire but first knock that snow off your fur."

Snow-white and Rose-red stroked the gentle bear until they went to bed.

"You are welcome to rest by the fire until morning," the mother told the bear.

Next day the bear ambled across the snow into the forest. But all that winter, he came back each night to warm himself and sleep by the cheery fire. At last spring came. The leaves turned green and the snow melted. The bear said to Snow-white: "I'm going away and I won't come back for the whole summer."

"Where are you going, dear bear?" she asked.

"I must stay inside the forest to look for my father's treasure. Wicked dwarfs stole it from me," he growled.

The girls were sorry he was going away for a long time. They unbolted the door and as the bear hurried out he tore a bit of his fur. Snow-white thought she saw something glistening underneath but she wasn't sure, and the bear ran away before she could take a good look.

Later, the girls went to collect firewood. They saw a big tree lying on the ground with many small branches for them to chop off. When they got nearer they saw that something was jumping up and down by the tree trunk. Was it a squirrel or a rabbit? As they moved closer they saw that it was a dwarf! He had a bad-tempered wrinkly face and a white beard as long as himself. Somehow the end of his beard had got caught in the tree. The angry little fellow was jumping backwards and forwards like a puppy on a lead. He glared at the girls with fiery red eyes and shouted: "What are you girls staring at? Can't you come and help me, you stupid creatures? Don't just stand there!"

"What has happened?" Rose-red asked politely.

"Don't ask silly questions," the little man said crossly. "If you must know, I was splitting some wood from this tree for my fire. I only use small pieces, not great big logs. I'd driven in a wedge very neatly when the wretched thing flew out. The split in the tree closed and I didn't have time to pull out my lovely white beard. Now it's trapped and I'm stuck!"

"We're sorry," Snow-white said, but both girls smiled a little because the shrivelled-up dwarf looked so funny.

"Don't stand there laughing at me, you nasty girls," he screeched. "Do something to help, and do it quickly!"

"Calm down," said Snow-white, "I'll help you."

She took her scissors out of her pocket and snipped off the tip of his beard. As soon as he was free, the dwarf bent down and snatched up a sack of gold which had been hidden under the tree roots. He swung the sack over his shoulder and went off without a word of thanks. Instead he grumbled:

"What rough children! Cutting off a piece of my beard."

Some time later, Snow-white and Rose-red went to a stream to catch fish for dinner. As they reached the water they saw that something like a large grasshopper was jumping and hopping along the bank. It looked ready to

jump into the stream so they ran to see what it could be. It was the dwarf again!

"Whatever are you doing?" asked Rose-red. "You'll be in the water if you're not careful."

"Stupid girl," the dwarf yelled. "Can't you see that this wretched fish is trying to pull me in?"

It seemed that he had been fishing and the wind had tangled his beard around his line just as a big fish had swallowed the hook. The dwarf pulled and the fish pulled. The fish was getting the better of it for the dwarf was almost in the water. In the nick of time the girls seized the dwarf. They held on and tried to untangle his beard. It was no use. The fish twisted and turned. The tangle grew worse so once more the scissors were brought out and the dwarf lost a little more of his beard! He was furious. His voice squeaked in anger:

"You toadstools! What a mess you've made of my face! First you cut off the tip and now you've cut off the best part of my beautiful beard. I shan't be able to show myself to the other dwarfs, I shall be so ashamed!"

He seized a sack of pearls hidden in the grass and again without a word of thanks, he disappeared.

Time passed. The girls were now young ladies as they walked to the town to buy laces and ribbons for their new dresses. They noticed a huge bird wheeling and turning in the air. Suddenly it swooped down and they heard a pitiful scream. They ran to the spot. An eagle had caught their old friend the dwarf in its talons! The girls had pity on him so they stretched up and caught hold of his coat. They tugged and pulled until the eagle opened its claws and let go. The frightened dwarf fell on the ground but as soon as he got back his breath he jumped up and looked all over himself. Then he bellowed at the sisters:

"You've torn my coat. Couldn't you have been more careful, clumsy creatures!" Without a word he disappeared behind a rock, taking a bag of jewels with him, this time.

The girls laughed at his bad temper and rude ways and went into the town and did their shopping. On their way home, in a lonely spot, they saw the dwarf standing on a rock. He hadn't expected anyone to come along so he had spread out his jewels. Green emeralds, fiery red rubies, pearls and white flashing diamonds all glittered and sparkled in the evening sun. They were so beautiful that the girls stopped to look at them.

"What are you doing here?" the dwarf screamed. His face reddened with anger and he shook his fist. He was still screaming when there was a deep growl and out from behind a rock a large bear ran up. The dwarf was terrified. He didn't have time to run away so he fell on his knees.

"Dear Mr Bear, spare my life," he begged. "You can take my rubies, pearls, emeralds and diamonds if you

like. Don't eat me. Eat these two big girls instead!"

The bear growled and with his front paw he gave the horrid dwarf a great blow which knocked him right over!

The frightened girls started to run away when they heard someone calling: "Snow-white! Rose-red! Wait for me, don't be afraid." They stopped. It was the bear who had warmed himself by their fire! As he drew near, the shaggy bearskin fell off and a handsome young man, dressed in scarlet and gold stood before them. "I am a king's son," he said, "that wicked dwarf stole my father's treasure and bewitched me. His spell has broken at last."

The prince went to visit his father and returned with his younger brother. The two brothers married the two sisters and their mother lived with them in their beautiful palace. There she planted her two rose-bushes which every summer covered themselves with roses – snow-white and rose-red!

THE SUNSHADE

There once lived a girl called Agatha whose father was a rich goldsmith. They lived in a grand house with many rooms filled with wonderful furniture and a lovely garden filled with flowers.

Agatha's cupboards were full of silk and satin dresses and she had boxes overflowing with gold rings, bracelets and necklaces. But they did not make her happy for Agatha was very ugly. She hated anyone to look at her so she stayed at home all day and wandered about the house. Sometimes she sat in the garden but she never went past the high garden walls until it was growing dark.

One day the cook in the goldsmith's house was ill.

"Agatha, my dear," her father said, "will you go to the market today to buy meat and vegetables?"

"Oh father," she exclaimed, "can't someone else go?"

"They are busy," he replied, "it won't take very long."

Agatha wanted to help her kind father so she went to the market. She tied a scarf round her neck, and pulled her bonnet down over her forehead to hide her ugly face.

The women in the market place turned and stared rudely.

"Look, that's Agatha, the goldsmith's daughter," they whispered, "she certainly is ugly!"

Poor Agatha went quickly from stall to stall. She heard the unkind whispering and she wanted to get home as soon as she could. Suddenly an old woman called out:

"Why are you in such a hurry, my dear? Come and look at my stall."

Her voice was kind and gentle so the girl stopped and turned around.

"There's something here I'd like to show you," the old woman said as she delved into the bottom of an old basket. She pulled out a sunshade and shook it open. "Isn't this beautiful?" she asked.

"Oh yes," replied Agatha, "this pretty blue is my favourite colour and I love the pearl and silver embroidery. But I do not need a sunshade, for I stay indoors most of the day."

"Hold it up," the old woman said sweetly, "then take a look at yourself." She held out a gleaming mirror. At first Agatha was frightened to look. Then she timidly held the glass and looked. A lovely face looked out at her!

"You see," chuckled the woman, "whenever you hold this sunshade over your head, the beauty which comes from your kind heart will be seen. Nobody will jeer at you again."

"I wish it were mine," sighed the girl.

"Take it, my child, I give it to you most gladly. Use it and be happy!"

Agatha took off her gold bracelet and handed it to her. "Please accept this in return and I hope it brings you happiness as well!"

She went on with her shopping and this time she pushed back her bonnet and smiled happily at the shopkeepers from under the pretty sunshade. When she got home she closed the sunshade and at once she saw her ugly face again in the mirror.

"I won't tell father about this," she decided, "he wouldn't like to see me beautiful and then ugly again."

She hid the sunshade in her room then carried the shopping down to the kitchen.

That evening Agatha put on a lovely silk dress and she went for a walk in the town. "I expect it looks silly carrying a sunshade at night but if it makes me beautiful, I don't care!" she said to herself. But nobody noticed. Instead, everybody admired her as she walked along and wondered who she was.

In the town centre there was a big park and every night a band played and coloured lights sparkled in the trees. Agatha had heard the music many times in her garden but she had never dared to go and dance before. Now she held up her sunshade and danced and whirled until she was out of breath. All the young men crowded round and begged her to dance with them. Agatha smiled for usually they would not even speak to her.

"Are you a visitor? Will you come riding with us? How long are you staying?" they demanded. Agatha wandered with her admirers through the gardens and round the lake. Her eyes sparkled and she was enjoying the jokes and chatter when she heard some jeering and cruel laughter.

Had she closed her sunshade? Had its magic gone away? Was she ugly again? She looked round and saw that a crowd had gathered round an old man with a crooked back.

"You ugly creature," they yelled, "get out of our town. We don't want you here."

Some men were pulling his jacket, one man tore off his cap and another kicked away the poor crooked man's stick.

"We must help him," said Agatha, "he can't hurt anyone and he can't help himself. Come along!" and she

pushed and elbowed her way through the crowd.

"Leave him alone," she called, "can't you see that he is small and helpless. Stop your bullying!"

"But he is ugly, a horrible old man," screamed a girl. Agatha was shocked. Quickly she held her sunshade over his head. And at once he stood up straight and tall. His face became young, his clothes were made from the finest cloth and his eyes twinkled with happiness. Everybody gasped in astonishment. What had happened to the ugly old man?

Agatha stepped back. She felt sure the crowd would laugh at her ugly face now. But they were so busy looking at the handsome young man that they took no notice of her. He was still holding the sunshade over his head for he didn't know what had changed him. Agatha wanted her sunshade back, but then thought it would be kinder to leave it with the man.

She left her friends and walked sadly across the park by herself. She rested for a minute by the lake and she bent down to touch the cool water. A beautiful face stared up at her. She could not believe it so she ran home and looked in the mirror. It was true!

She was not ugly any more for her kind heart and her good deed had made her truly beautiful.

THE THREE LITTLE PIGS

Once upon a time there were three little pigs. One day they set out from the farm where they had been born. They were going out into the world to start new lives and enjoy any adventures that might come their way.

The first little pig met a man carrying some straw, and he asked him if he might have some to build himself a house.

"Of course, little pig," said the man. He gave the little pig a big bundle of straw, and the little pig built himself a lovely house of golden straw.

A big bad wolf lived nearby. He came along and saw the new house and, feeling rather hungry and thinking he would like to eat a little pig for supper, he called out,

"Little pig, little pig, let me come in." To which the little pig replied,

"No, no, by the hair of my chinny chin chin,

I'll not let you in!"

So the wolf shouted very crossly,

"Then I'll huff and I'll puff,

Till I blow your house in!"

And he huffed and he puffed, and he HUFFED and he PUFFED until the house of straw fell in, and the wolf ate the little pig for his supper that evening.

The second little pig was walking along the road when he met a man with a load of wood. "Please Sir," he said, "can you let me have some of that wood so that I can build a house?"

"Of course," said the man, and he gave him a big pile of wood. In no time at all, the little pig had built himself a lovely house. The next evening, along came the same wolf. When he saw another little pig, this time in a wooden house, he called out,

"Little pig, little pig, let me come in."
To which the pig replied,
"No, no, by the hair of my chinny chin chin,
I'll not let you in!"
So the wolf shouted,
"Then I'll huff and I'll puff,
Till I blow your house in!"
And he huffed and he puffed and he HUFFED and he PUFFED until the house fell in and the wolf gobbled up the little pig for his supper.

The third little pig met a man with a cartload of bricks. "Please Sir, can I have some bricks to build myself a house?" he asked, and when the man had given him some, he built himself a lovely house with the bricks.

The big bad wolf came along, and licked his lips as he thought about the third little pig. He called out,
"Little pig, little pig, let me come in!"
And the little pig called back,
"No, no, by the hair of my chinny chin chin,
I'll not let you in!"
So the wolf shouted,
"Then I'll huff and I'll puff,
Till I blow your house in!"
And the wolf huffed and he puffed, and he HUFFED and he PUFFED, and he HUFFED again and PUFFED again, but still the house, which had been so well built with bricks, did not blow in.

The wolf went away to think how he could trick the

little pig, and he came back and called through the
window of the brick house, "Little pig, there are some
marvellous turnips in the farmer's field. Shall we go there
tomorrow morning at six o'clock and get some?"

The little pig thought this was a very good idea, as he
was very fond of turnips, but he went at five o'clock, not
six o'clock, and collected all the turnips he needed before
the wolf arrived.

The wolf was furious, but he thought he would try
another trick. He told the little pig about the apples in the
farmer's orchard, and suggested they both went to get
some at five o'clock the next morning. The little pig
agreed, and went as before, an hour earlier. But this time

the wolf came early too, and arrived while the little pig was still in the apple tree. The little pig pretended to be pleased to see him and threw an apple down to the wolf. While the wolf was picking it up, the little pig jumped down the tree and got into a barrel. He rolled quickly down the hill inside this barrel to his house of bricks and rushed in and bolted the door.

The wolf was very angry that the little pig had got the better of him again, and chased him in the barrel back to his house. When he got there he climbed on to the roof, intending to come down the chimney and catch the little pig that way. The little pig was waiting for him, however, with a large cauldron of boiling water on the fire. The wolf came down the chimney and fell into the cauldron with a big SPLASH, and the little pig quickly put the lid on it.

The wicked wolf was never seen again, and the little pig lived happily in his brick house for many many years.

THE FIVE SERVANTS

In a country thousands of miles away, there once lived a queen who lived in a wonderful palace. She was mean and bad-tempered, but her daughter was good and beautiful.

The queen ordered that any prince who wanted to marry the princess should first pass three special tests in order to win her hand. If he failed, his head would be chopped off.

One day a handsome prince asked his father to let him try for the hand of the lovely princess.

"It is dangerous, my son," said the king, "that wicked queen may kill you."

"Please let me go," replied his son, "I will be careful and I'm sure I can win the princess for my wife."

So he travelled for many days over the mountains until one day when he was riding through the forest he saw an enormous man lying under a tree. He was twice as big as ten bulls put together!

"Do you want a good servant?" he said to the prince.

"You are too fat to help me," the prince replied.

"I'm cheerful and honest so my size doesn't matter!"

"Come along then," said the prince and they went on through the forest until they saw another man lying with his ear on the grass.

"What are you doing?" asked the fat man.

"I'm listening to every sound in the world," was the answer, "I can even hear grass growing."

"Alright," laughed the prince. "Tell me what you can

hear at the queen's palace,"

"I hear the *swoosh* of a sword. It is cutting off the head of a prince."

"You will be useful, I can see," said the prince, "so come along with me."

They had not gone very far when they saw a pair of feet, then they walked a long way until they saw a man's body. They had to walk further on until they reached his head!

"You're as long as a river," said the listening man.

"Oh," said the tall man, "when I stretch, I am as high as three mountains!"

"I'm sure you will be useful," said the prince, "so come along with me."

The four went merrily on until they saw a man sitting in the sun, but he was shivering and shaking.

"Why are you shivering in this lovely warm sun?" the

tall man asked.

"Oh dear, the sun makes me shiver with cold and the ice and snow make me warm and cosy," the man said.

"How strange," the prince said, "if you like, you may come along with us."

Next, they met a man who was looking everywhere with his neck stretched out.

"What are you looking for?" the frosty man asked.

"I have sharp eyes and I can see over fields and mountains everywhere in the world," he replied.

"That's useful," said the prince. "You'd better come with me."

They travelled together until they reached the city where the queen and her daughter lived. The prince went to the palace and said to the queen:

"What must I do to win the princess?"

"I will give you three tasks," the queen replied, "and

if you do them properly, you may marry my daughter. First, you must find the ring I lost in the middle of the sea.''

The prince returned to his five friends. "I must find a ring. Can you help me, please?"

"I will find out where in the sea it is hidden," said the sharp-eyed man, and he looked over mountains until he spied the sea. "It is lying on a rock," he said.

"I will get it if only I can see it," said the tall man.

"I can help you," said the fat man and he drank up all the water in the sea.

The rock was easy to find now and the tall man stretched out his long arm and picked up the ring. He handed it to the prince who carried it to the palace and gave it to the queen.

"It is my ring," she said slowly, "but you must do the second task now." She took him to the window and showed him the meadows below.

"There are a hundred oxen there and you must eat them by twelve o'clock. But that's not all. In the cellar there are a hundred barrels of wine and you must drink every drop."

"Can I invite a friend to share the feast?" he asked.

"You may invite one guest," the queen laughed nastily, "and only one."

The prince talked to his friends again. "I think you are the best one to help me," he told the fat man, "and you will be able to eat as much as you like."

So the next day the two of them went to the meadow. The fat man ate the hundred oxen without leaving a crumb. "Is that all I'm getting for breakfast today?" he asked. "I need a drink now."

The prince led him to the cellar where he drank all the wine without spilling a single drop.

"My guest and I have enjoyed our meal," the prince told the queen, "and now I'm ready for the third task."

The queen was angry. Nobody had managed to do even one task before. "I'll chop off this prince's head before long," she muttered. Then she said to the prince: "Tonight I will bring my daughter to your house. I'll leave her with you and you must not leave her side. And you must not go to sleep either. When the clock strikes twelve I'll come to collect her. If she is not sitting there at that time, you will die."

The prince returned to his friends.

"This time I have an easy job," he told them.

"I only have to keep my eyes open and sit by the princess. Still, I do not trust the queen. She'll try and play

a trick on me so, my friends, will you help me again? We do not want her to get away."

When it was dark, the queen brought her daughter to the prince's house. At once the listening man put his ear to the floor, the tall man twisted himself round the house, the sharp-eyed man watched over the city and the fat man sat by the door so that nobody could move past him.

The prince looked at the beautiful princess in the moonlight and straightaway he fell in love with her. He wanted to marry her more than ever so he watched her very closely.

But at eleven o'clock the wicked queen cast a magic spell over the prince and his servants. They fell asleep and at that moment, the princess vanished. But the queen had not said the words properly so the spell finished at a quarter to midnight. The friends woke up with a start. "The princess has gone!" the prince cried, "I haven't finished the three tasks, so the queen will cut off my head."

They fell quiet until the listening man said: "I will listen and see if I can hear the princess." He waited a minute then he said: "She is sitting crying somewhere."

The sharp-eyed man said: "She is sitting on a rock three hundred miles away."

"I can reach her with two steps," the tall man cried. And before the others could blink an eye, he had reached the rock, picked up the girl and carried her back to the prince's house.

They were laughing happily when the queen arrived at twelve o'clock. She was furious! She had to admit that the prince had completed the three tasks she had set, but she said that he must do one more before he could take the princess as his wife.

So, the next day the queen told her servants to bring a thousand logs. When they were piled up, she turned to the prince and said: "This is my final test for you. I want someone to sit on those logs when they are burning fiercely."

The friends heard this and they turned to the frosty-man. "We have already helped the prince," they said, "it is your turn now," and they helped him to sit on the logs. Then they set them on fire. The frosty-man shivered and shook until the logs were all burnt then he walked out from the ashes. "*Brr*," he said, "I'm freezing! I've never shivered so much in my life!"

The queen agreed at last to her daughter marrying the prince the next day. But in secret she ordered her soldiers to capture the prince and bring back the princess. Luckily, the listening man pricked up his ears and heard the queen's wicked plan.

So, the couple hurried off to the church with the five special friends, and were married before the queen could stop the wedding.

The prince gave his friends a big reward for their help and they went on their travels. He took the princess to his own country and the king held a big wedding feast for them. The prince had won the princess and they lived in great happiness ever after.

THE NUTCRACKER

One hundred years ago on Christmas Eve, a little girl called Clara and her brother Fritz were having a party at their house. The room was bright with candles and the fire crackled cheerfully, as grown-ups and children joined together in all the games and dances.

Clara's eyes shone. "Isn't this lovely?" she whispered to the little wooden nutcracker hidden in her handkerchief. It was a Christmas present from her godfather.

"Look closely at the wooden head," he said as he gave it to her. "This is no ordinary nutcracker."

"His face is very sad," Clara thought, "but I like it." And from that moment she carried the little nutcracker doll with her everywhere.

"Bang, bang!" cried Fritz, who was drilling his new toy soldiers. "My soldiers are brave and handsome. Better than your ugly little doll."

"Take no notice of him," Clara said to the nutcracker. "He doesn't mean to be unkind." But the noise in the hot, crowded room made Fritz very excited. He marched up to Clara, snatched the little nutcracker and held it above his head.

"Catch it if you can!" he yelled, dancing up and down. Clara tried to grab his arm but naughty Fritz hurled the little wooden doll across the room where it landed near the Christmas tree. Just then Clara's mother came up to her.

"It's supper time, Clara; come and help me," she

said, and poor Clara had to leave her new toy where it had fallen.

Much later, the party was over and the children's friends went home, calling "Happy Christmas!" to each other through the snow. Clara and Fritz went to bed and it was not long before everyone in the house was asleep – everyone except Clara. She could not bear to leave the little nutcracker alone, so she crept downstairs and opened the sitting room door.

What a sight met her eyes! There were mice running everywhere, fighting and biting, and chewing all the presents under the Christmas tree! As Clara gazed in horror, she heard someone calling,

"Over here, men! Ready to charge!" It was the little nutcracker, leading the toy soldiers into battle against the mice.

"Oh good!" Clara cheered. "Don't let the mice spoil everything."

Suddenly a huge mouse wearing a golden crown leapt forward. It was the Mouse King himself, waving a sword of shining steel. The wooden swords of the toy soldiers were powerless against it and the Nutcracker had no sword at all. In a flash, Clara tore off her slipper and threw it across the room as hard as she could. It hit the Mouse King and he dropped his sword. The Nutcracker seized it, and with one stroke he cut off the King's head. At once, the other mice stopped fighting and scurried away to their holes.

Clara turned – to find that her ugly little Nutcracker had been transformed into a handsome prince dressed in silver and white. He smiled down at her, "You've saved my life and broken a wicked spell, little Clara. Now I am free to go back to my own country at last."

Then the prince sat Clara down under the Christmas tree and told her of his adventures.

Once upon a time, his story began, a queen quarrelled with all the mice in her palace and banished them from her kingdom. As he slunk out of the hall, a wicked old wizard mouse turned to the queen and squeaked,

"You'll be sorry for this – and so will your daughter." The queen ran to her baby's crib, but too late. The baby's tiny cheeks were thin and hairy and whiskers grew under her pointed nose. She had been turned into a rat!

The grief-stricken queen called all the wisest men in her kingdom together, and they studied their magic

books till they came upon a way to break the wizard mouse's spell. A Krakatuk tree must be found, and one of its nuts must be picked. Then someone strong enough must crack open the nut and give the kernel to the rat princess. As soon as she ate it, the spell would be broken. The wise men searched. All the queen's subjects searched. At long last they found a Krakatuk tree nut and a young prince to open it. Crack, crack. He split the shell and gave the Krakatuk nut to the rat princess. She ate it, and instantly became a little baby again.

"Oh thank you, thank you," cried the queen. But as she spoke the prince grew smaller and smaller, until he had turned into a little wooden nutcracker. They heard the wizard mouse squeaking with laughter, "You may have your princess back, but you've lost the prince, and one day King Mouse will cut off his head!"

216

"So I became an ugly little nutcracker," the prince went on. "One day your godfather found me. He was sure you wouldn't mind my ugly face, Clara, and he was right. Thank you for saving my life . . . I must return to my own country now, so would you like to come with me to the Kingdom of Sweets and visit my Sugar Palace?"

Clara was too excited to speak, but she nodded, her eyes shining. At once the Christmas tree grew taller and taller and its lights glittered like bright stars. The walls of the sitting room disappeared. Clara and the prince were floating in the shimmering moonlight in a walnut-shell boat. Around them, snowflake fairies danced to sweet music and gently guided the boat to the shore of Candyland. The prince and Clara stepped out and walked up an avenue of trees laden with toffee apples, glittering sugar plums and chocolate nuts. They passed cottages whose walls were chocolate bars, with barley-sugar windows. The breezes smelt of honey and strawberry jam.

"It's . . . it's delicious," Clara whispered, her eyes darting here, there and everywhere. The nutcracker prince laughed,

"Wait until you see my palace!" And he pointed through the trees to a mass of glittering towers. A beautiful Sugar Plum Fairy came towards them and smiled at Clara.

"My snowflake fairies have told me what you did, and I want to thank you for saving our prince." She led the little girl to a magnificent throne inside the palace. "Tonight you are Queen Clara!"

Then the celebrations began. Sugar sticks twirled, chocolate drop cymbals clashed. A Chinese teapot and a set of Arabian coffee cups waltzed together, a troupe of

Cossacks leapt across the floor. Spun-sugar roses curtsied gracefully as the prince invited the Sugar Plum Fairy to dance. How all the people clapped and cheered!

"Welcome to our prince," they cried. "Hurrah for the Nutcracker! Hurrah for Clara! Hurrah! Hurrah!"

Clara blinked; her eyes were dazzled.

"Hurrah! It's Christmas Day," she heard her brother Fritz shouting as she opened her eyes. The dancers, the Sugar Plum Fairy and the prince were all gone, and not a trace of the Sugar Palace remained.

"It must have been a dream," thought Clara sadly.

Time passed, and Clara quite forgot the little nutcracker.

But many years later, on her wedding day, she smiled a secret smile because the sugary towers of the wedding cake reminded her of the prince's palace and, on the top, she was sure she glimpsed a tiny sugar plum fairy dancing.

THE RESCUE OF WILL SCARLETT

In Sherwood Forest near Nottingham a man called Robin Hood lived with his band of Merry Men. They wore green jerkins and they spent their time helping poor and hungry people. The rich barons and the Sheriff of Nottingham hated them for Robin took their gold and gave it away to the poor. So one day they sent their soldiers into Sherwood Forest to hunt for him and they managed to capture Robin's great friend, Will Scarlett. They flung him into a dark dungeon at Guy of Gisborne's castle. Robin and his men sat round their camp-fire, wondering how to rescue Will. Suddenly, Much the Miller ran breathlessly into the camp.

"Bad news, Robin," he gasped. "Kate, a kitchen maid at the castle tells me that Will is to be hanged tomorrow! And five guards watch over him night and day."

"That is not good," sighed Robin, "but we must get into the dungeon somehow. How can we do that?"

"Kate takes food to Will," said Much the Miller slowly. "I think she would take a message to him."

"You've given me an idea, Much," said Robin. "One of us must take that message!"

"How can that be? It is impossible. The guards would spot our green jerkins," the men cried out.

"Much," said Robin. "This girl, Kate. Is she a friend of yours?"

"Aye, Robin," Much smiled. "One day forsooth we'll get married."

"Well then," said Robin. "You and Kate must change places tonight. Then you can carry Will's food and cut him loose. Somehow you must then open the castle gate. We will be waiting outside for you."

"But Robin, I don't look like a girl. I'm much bigger than Kate!" Poor Much did not like this plan.

"With a cap and shawl and long skirts, no one will know you, Much." Little John said. "But what about the girl, Robin? We cannot have two Kates in the castle!"

"I will bring her safely here," said Friar Tuck, "do not worry about her."

"To work, men, for it will soon be dark," cried Robin. "Much, take and hide these daggers under your dress.

Men, sharpen your arrows then away we go!"

Out of the forest they rode. They hid their horses near the castle and crept quietly towards the castle walls.

Much walked boldly inside. The guards knew him because every day he carried great sacks of flour to the kitchen. He walked on with the daggers inside his flour covered jerkin.

"Kate," he called and she ran to greet him. "Kate," he whispered, "Are you willing to help the poor prisoner, Will Scarlett?"

"Oh no, no," she said, "I'm too frightened of the baron and his guards."

"Will is not a wicked man," Much told her, "but one who helps the poor. Robin Hood and his men are waiting outside but we need your help."

"Robin Hood!" Kate's eyes opened wide. Who had *not* heard of him and his good deeds!

"The prisoner seems to be kind and gentle," she said slowly, "but how can a kitchen maid help him?"

Much told her about Robin's plan.

"You – a girl!" Kate giggled, "But what about me?"

"Friar Tuck will take you to the forest. You'll be safe there. Now, what time do you take food to the dungeon?"

"Nine o'clock. But I'm not sure . . ."

Much took her hand. "You'll be helping the poor and the hungry. Will is Robin's friend and a true friend of the king's. You must help."

"I'll do it. I'll help you," and she squeezed his hand.

They changed clothes. Kate tied a scarf round Much's head and she threw a huge apron over his skirts.

"You'll have to take off those boots," she declared, "I hope no one looks at your feet. And Much, try not to take such big steps! Walk like this . . ." She showed him how to walk and where to go then she slipped outside the gate before it was closed for the night.

"Kate, where are you?" shouted one of the guards. "Bring some ale!" Much dared not speak so he grabbed a jug, put it on the table, picked up a plate of food and started on the journey to the dungeons. His scarf slipped and what with holding the plate, hiding his face and trying not to trip over his skirts, poor Much grew hotter and hotter.

He reached the steps leading down to the dungeon. He heard the clash of armour so he pressed himself against the wall. To his horror it was the cruel baron, Guy of Gisborne, himself. Much was terrified but he managed to do a half-curtsey as the baron swept past him!

At last, Much reached the dungeon door. He was trembling as he gave a timid knock – not his usual thump!

"That's the last food the prisoner gets before he is hanged," the guard said as he swung open the door and allowed Much in.

He scurried down the stone stairs and tiptoed to the man lying on some straw.

"Do not move," he whispered, "It is I, Much the Miller."

"Much? Is it really you?" Will muttered, unable to believe his eyes. "I knew Robin would rescue me!"

"Well, I got in here alright but we still have to get out," said Much. "This is the plan. You hide behind these skirts and I'll stumble on the steps. The guards will turn round and we'll threaten them with these." He handed two daggers to Will from under his skirt.

Slowly and carefully they went up the stairs and the guards seeing 'Kate', started to unfasten the door. Much

caught his foot in his skirt and dropped the plate which broke into a thousand pieces.

The guards rushed to see what the noise was all about and Will immediately stood up, daggers in his hands. The astonished guards were soon bundled away and shut up in their own dungeon!

Will and Much crept across the hall, through the kitchen and were opening the door when a soldier saw Much. He quickly grabbed a jug of ale and threw it over him. The soldier spluttered and gasped while Much and Will sped across the courtyard to the castle gate.

In the meantime Robin and his men had gathered outside the castle. Suddenly there were shouts of rage and lights appeared. "Get ready, men," yelled Robin. And they fitted sharp arrows into their bows.

Much and Will struggled with the iron bar on the huge gate while soldiers swarmed out behind them. Robin's men fired their arrows and made the soldiers take shelter.

As soon as the gate opened, Robin seized Will, and Little John grabbed Much by his skirts and they threw them both over two horses. "Back to Sherwood Forest, men," ordered Robin. They rode away, shouting joyfully. Will Scarlett had been saved! Little John said Much the Miller was the heaviest girl he had ever carried and Much himself married the brave kitchen maid, Kate.